pretty

pretty
stories

GREG KEARNEY

Library and Archives Canada Cataloguing in Publication

Kearney, Greg
    Pretty : stories / Greg Kearney.

ISBN 978-1-55096-220-8

    I. Title.

PS8621.E23P74 2011   C813'.6   C2011-901509-9

Design and Composition by Digital ReproSet mc
Cover Designed by John Webster
Typeset in Big Caslon at the Moons of Jupiter Studios
Printed by Imprimerie Gauvin

The publisher would like to acknowledge the financial assistance of
the Canada Council for the Arts and the Ontario Arts Council, which is
an agency of the Government of Ontario.

 Conseil des Arts   Canada Council    ONTARIO ARTS COUNCIL
du Canada   for the Arts   CONSEIL DES ARTS DE L'ONTARIO

Printed and Bound in Canada in 2011
Published by Exile Editions Ltd.
144483 Southgate Road 14 – GD
Holstein, Ontario, N0G 2A0

Canadian Sales Distribution: U.S. Sales Distribution:
McArthur & Company   Independent Publishers Group
c/o Harper Collins   814 North Franklin Street
1995 Markham Road   Chicago, IL 60610
Toronto, ON M1B 5M8   www.ipgbook.com
toll free: 1 800 387 0117   toll free: 1 800 888 4741

For Robert Matte, naturally.

contents

"I felt a girl who wanted to be too beautiful. I felt a mother who wanted to love her. I felt a demon who wanted to torture her. I felt them mixed together so you couldn't tell them apart."

—MARY GAITSKILL, *Veronica*

Mary
Steenburgen

It was almost midnight, and none of them had really had a proper dinner yet. So, right after her husband came in the cleaning woman's eye, Denise wrapped herself in a bathrobe, double-knotted the belt, and went into the kitchen. She cut up some dill pickles. Then she made a mound of sandwiches from the previous night's roast beef.

Weak and mildly tachycardic after his orgasm, Cliff felt his way along the kitchen wall, leaning. He'd lost 90 pounds since the heart attack. The leftover skin – his buttocks hung like ancient drapes.

"Cover up, for God's sake," Denise said in the kitchen.

Cliff sighed a fake sigh. "Wasn't that great," he said.

"Yeah. Really great."

Denise tried to stack the sandwiches in an artful way. She thought of her tentative tongue-kissing with Clara, this woman. Clara's vast areolas. She'd never seen Cliff so excited. About anything. Ever.

Denise put the tray of sandwiches on the living room coffee table. Cliff put on a CD. The best of Styx. Denise cleared her throat. She winced at the thought of tomorrow's workday. She made a mental note to remember to leave her workspace spotless, empty her own garbage. Lighten the load for Clara, the new cleaning woman at the office. It was the least she could do.

Cliff had actually suggested paying her, Clara, for the three-way, when Denise was still planning things. But Denise knew that Clara would never accept money. And she lived with her mother, so her living expenses were minimal anyway. Of course, she could have as many sandwiches as she wanted, and one of them would drive her to the subway, no problem.

Clara came into the living room, fully dressed. She said something but the Styx was cranked, drowning her out. Denise screamed at Cliff to turn the music down.

"Hi," Clara said. "Thank you for having me over."

Denise smiled, looking at the gold-framed painting of her dead dog on the wall above the stereo.

"Of course," Denise said. "Thank *you* for coming over. Have a sandwich."

Cliff wrapped his arms around Clara from behind.

"I've got another kind of sandwich in mind," Cliff said.

"Cliff," Denise said. "The moment has passed."

"I love sandwiches," Clara said, taking a sandwich. "I'm in love with sandwiches!"

Denise went to the bathroom. Cliff tried to chat with Clara. Clara mumbled things, her mouth full of sandwich.

When Cliff was near death, he made Denise promise him a few things. If he died, she should try to keep the house going and not buy a condo. She could remarry, but only if the guy was shorter than Cliff and made less money than Cliff did.

Denise loved Cliff. The thought of his death bore a jagged bolt down the middle of her.

If he survived, he wanted to put a tanning bed in the basement. He wanted to be more sexually adventurous, have three-ways, go to swingers' parties, try it up the ass with Denise.

"Yes, yes, sure, yes," Denise said at the time, petting his puffy palm.

As her February fake bake and anal fissure could attest, Denise held to her word. And now they'd had the three-way. Cliff enjoyed it; Denise had not. It was forced, slightly sad, poorly lit, Denise recalled, as she rose from the bed after Cliff came, thinking that the whole tableau resembled a crime scene photograph.

Maybe if they'd picked a stranger. Or a really pretty prostitute. One who looked like Mary Steenburgen. Denise had always found her attractive.

She sat on the toilet, going over her reluctant, gummy seduction of the slightly stupid cleaning lady. The Tim Hortons tea biscuits. The vague promise of a desk job. Bingo, even. Bingo, where Clara screamed "I've got fuckin' Bingo!" so maniacally that Denise instinctively ducked under the table.

Poor Clara. Denise felt like she should give money to a relevant charity now that her husband had come in Clara's eye. But she couldn't think of a relevant charity.

+

"It's always soo nice to make new friends," Clara said, swaying to Styx's "Babe."

"Absolutely," Cliff said. "Hey, Clara...have you... have you ever done cocaine?

Denise hurled the *Canadian Living* she was skimming across the living room.

"Good Christ, Cliff! Enough is enough. It's after midnight! God. God. This isn't us. I missed Jay Leno. Please let's just...I'm sorry, Clara."

Clara laughed.

"No problemo. Hey. Really. No problemo at all. My last old man and me, we used to party all the time. I still like to party. Love it. Someone asks me what I want to be in my wildest dreams, I say I want to be all fucked up on killer shit! That would be so wild. I'd be super happy. My mum wouldn't like it. She says I'm going to hell because I like colourful panties. So. Hey! I got a little piece in my purse, a little rock. You guys wanna party a little?"

"We don't go in for that," Denise said. "Thank you, though."

"Well," Cliff said. "I might as well try a pinch."

"A pinch!" Denise sneered. "It's not oregano, you know. Cliff. Cliff. You have a 9:15 appointment with Dr. Brennan in the morning. In nine hours, to be exact."

"Denise, clam up for awhile, 'kay?"

"Nice," Clara said. "Nice! This is so wild."

Denise looked at her husband. She slept at the foot of his hospital bed, night after night. Got to know all the nurses. One of them offered to pray with her. She prayed, hand in hand, with a very old Catholic nurse over Cliff, in his coma, in the hospital.

Now she watched as Clara drew a glass pipe from her purse and Cliff clapped his hands like a toddler on his birthday.

If Cliff dropped dead doing drugs with Clara, Denise would not be held accountable. She would not be held accountable, and she would not care. She would let Clara call 911.

How was she going to get hard-drug stench out of the upholstery? With book club at her house that Wednesday? Maybe Clara the Cracked-Out Cleaning Lady would have a few tips.

Cliff told Clara that she could stay the night. Behind her, Denise gestured wildly, wanting Cliff to immediately rescind the offer. Too late. Clara accepted. Denise stormed off to the guest bedroom, leaving Cliff and Clara to their druggy ruminations.

She lay in the dark on the hard single guest bedroom bed. What had happened to the man who proposed to her on a burry glen in Scotland? The man who said he understood and admired the fact that literature and curling were more important to her than children? Had she grown stodgy? Would the sensualist she proclaimed herself to be have stayed up and smoked crack with Clara?

Death. Cliff had come close to death, and he continued to live like a dying man. Denise wanted to live alongside Cliff, freewheeling, but she couldn't pretend she was dying. She was a tall, tidy woman; her nail beds were vermillion, her face ruddy, she took stairs two, even three at a time. She wanted to have fun, but she couldn't pretend decadence. Her slow, small, perfect pulse refuted it.

Her mind whirred. She considered taking half an Ativan. Instead she got up, re-tied her housecoat, went back into the living room.

"Woo!" Clara hooted. "She's back in business! Come and sit."

"Yeah, no. It really is time that we wrap things up, Clara. Again, thank you so much."

"But Denise," Cliff said, shivering. "I've just smoked crack."

"That's so great. I'll be right back."

Denise went to the kitchen for her purse. She pulled out all the bills in her wallet: three tens and a twenty. She called Clara into the kitchen.

"Hey," said Clara in the kitchen. "It's the right time of the night! 'It's the Right Time of the Night' – who sang that song? I love that song."

"Jennifer Warnes, if I'm not mistaken. Now, here's some money for a taxi. I'm calling Co-Op Cabs. One should be along in five minutes."

"I don't want to go home. I just started to party."

Phone in hand, Denise fixed Clara with a look she used to use on her dog when he was being obstinate. Clara clammed up and followed Denise into the foyer. They waited there, not speaking, until the cab arrived.

Cliff was dancing robotically to "Mr. Roboto" when Denise returned to the living room. Denise gave him the "bad dog" glare and he, too, stopped what he was doing.

She turned off the stereo. She gestured at the couch; he sat.

"We need to talk," she said.

"I'm sorry I smoked crack," he said. "It seemed like the thing to do. I didn't want to be elitist. But I'll never do it again. I feel awful. Terrible tachycardia."

"If you ever smoke crack again, our marriage is over. But that's not what I want to talk about. Three-ways..."

Cliff put up his hand, certain of what Denise was about to say.

"That's it for three-ways, too. I've had my fun, really."

Denise shushed Cliff.

"When next we have a three-way, I don't want to have to do all the legwork. I'm not going to get all panicky trying to please you, picking the first person I see. We'll find someone online, vet them *thoroughly*, *together*, and then arrange a nice, elegant encounter. Also, if the third person is female – "

"*If* the third person is female?"

"If you can try crack, you can try dick. Anyway, if the third person is female, I have a very specific type of woman I'm attracted to. I'm not going to eat out any old, blank-eyed drug casualty like I did tonight."

With Cliff hopped up on crack, Denise realized that she could now proceed to describe, in minute detail, the kind of woman she wanted, and Cliff would be unable to cite fatigue and beg off.

So Denise went on and on about what kind of woman she liked, surprising herself at her particularity: small hands, real nails, unfussy brows, B-cup breasts, ample buttocks, dark, curly hair like Mary Steenburgen's, a crinkly smile like Mary Steenburgen's...

Denise found herself getting excited as the sexy archetype took shape. She looked over at Cliff; he was taking his pulse, alternately at the wrist and throat.

She hoped that he would be okay. She hoped that he would survive, at least until the next three-way.

WHAT TO WEAR

I can't – I cannot – wear what I'm wearing to meet my sister.

I pivot in the mirror. I try different poses. Laconically slouched. Balletically balanced, chest out and shoulders back. It doesn't matter. I still look like hell.

From the neck up is okay. My hair is buzzed down to bristle. My face is angular, hollow-cheeked. So that's all fine and good. From the neck up, I look like an elite athlete. But from the neck down, well. That's another thing altogether.

This T-shirt exposes my thin, vascular arms. It clings to my round, hard gut that juts out at impossible angles. Looks like I'm smuggling an oven. I'm trying to think – do I own a poncho? Do I dare wear a poncho? Jutting gut or poncho? Jutting gut or poncho? It's such a "Sophie's Choice."

The last time my sister saw me, eight years ago, I had a perfect body, a waterfront condo, a daily column in the city's best and biggest newspaper, two nervous Weimaraners, and a beautiful Spanish boyfriend who was prone to rectal prolapse. I'm sure Sheila didn't know that last bit about the prolapse, unless Javier told her. They really hit it off, and Javier only knew a handful of English words and phrases. *That is interesting. I am fine. Herpes. How dare you!* And, of course, *rectal prolapse.* So I guess it might have slipped out in conversation. In any case, Sheila worshipped me, and was envious of all that I had.

Back then, Sheila was trying to be an actress. She had played the Diane Keaton part in *Crimes of the Heart,* her last year of theatre school. A talent agent saw her performance and took her on as a client. The agent sent her out on countless auditions, but Sheila never got work. Supposedly her agent said that the casting people invariably said that Sheila looked "too intellectual," even though she isn't intellectual. At all.

Floundering, Sheila asked me if she could borrow some money. I immediately agreed. I've always helped her out. Our mother died young and our father is an iceberg, so I've always felt responsible for her.

I asked why she needed money. She said she *had* to get a nose job. She said her life would be worthless if she didn't get a nose job.

We were standing around the marble island in my old kitchen. "A nose job," I said aloud. Javier nodded understandingly, understanding nothing. I looked heavenward, pondering.

"I'm sorry," I said. "I can't facilitate self-mutilation."

"But it's not self-mutilation," Sheila said. "A doctor will be doing it, not me."

"I'm sorry. Way too many gay men have been responsible for making women look ridiculous. I have to buck the trend."

"It's not a trend. It's my life. It's my livelihood."

"I'm sorry, Sheila. I don't agree with cosmetic surgery. Period."

"Fine. You can be a rich fag with everything, and I'll just fucking die. In the gutter."

She stormed out. I called and called, for several months. She never picked up, never called back. What more could I do? I was saddened, I missed her – perhaps her total independence was for the best.

I got shingles, all down the right side of my chest, so bad it made my doctor wince. He tested me for HIV; it came back positive. And I only had 205 T cells. He put me on the cocktail. It made me sick for months. I had no health insurance. I burned through all my savings. Javier literally went out for milk and never came back. I sold the condo.

An AIDS Committee volunteer, this nice older woman, ran errands for me and walked Ike and Tina, my dogs. I had never really bonded with them. They were always so yappy and frenetic, and now that I was sick I just wanted to drown them. So I asked the woman if she wanted them. They seemed to like her better anyway. She took them and renamed Ike Marty.

Marty and Tina. They sound like Palm Springs swingers. But supposedly Marty comes when she calls.

So here I am, getting by on disability, living in a co-op that houses poor people with HIV. And I stand, before my mirror, assessing my body in fluorescent light. The meds caused lipodystrophy, sucking the fat from my face and arms and legs and plopping it on my midsection. I feel like a monster. I mean, I am glad that I survived. I just don't want to look so blatantly like a survivor.

+

I am a member of an internet dating site for men with HIV.

After months of silently lurking, a few weeks ago, I started chatting online with a guy in my area. Twenty-six, a chef, good grammar and spelling. He sent me a pic – cute as a button. I sent him a pic that I took of myself last year, black-and-white, head and shoulders. He wrote back right away, said I was handsome. We agreed to meet. At Woody's. I'll be the one in the black-and-white striped sweater, I wrote.

I was early. I had two pints before I saw him. He looked at me. Kept on walking. Seemed to circle the bar. I was sure he'd leave. But he came back to my table and said hello. He was wearing a pendant made from a hearing aid.

"Are you Ron?" he said.

"Hi," I said. "Kieran?"

"How's it going?"

"Good. Can I get you a drink?"

"Oh. No. That's okay. Thanks." He took a stool and sat. Smiled at me. Stopped smiling, abruptly.

"So," I said. "I like your necklace. Where did you get it?"

"A friend made it."

"Oh. Anyone I might have heard of?"

He did his smiling/stop smiling thing again. "Listen," he said. "I'm a very candid person."

"Good," I said. "That's a good way to be."

"Yeah. So. I have to say. I'm looking for someone who's kind of...how do I say it?"

"Candidly?" I said.

"I'm looking for someone who's kind of at the same stage of the journey. You know?"

"Oh. You said in your ad that you were looking for someone older."

"Yeah. No. I am. I guess I should say that I'm looking for someone at the same stage of the HIV journey."

"Oh. What stage are you at?"

His eyes scanned the ceiling. "You know. I'm totally healthy. And happy. And, you know, unhindered. In any way. By HIV."

"Me, too."

"Right. But you've, I think, had it longer than me."

"Yeah. Probably."

"And you had to take some of the earlier drugs."

"I don't know. Yeah."

"Right. So I haven't had to deal with that. With the earlier drugs and the – you know. Deformity or whatever."

He said *deformity*. I tried to be radiant and smile sagely, inured to insult. But I wanted to kick his head in. I had perceived myself as weathered. Grizzled, maybe. But deformed?

Am I deformed?

Say I'm deformed. Am I unequivocally, empirically deformed? Or is deformity a mutable thing, its official definition changing over time? Is deformity sexy, sometimes?

This is the dreck that keeps me up at night. I was handsome. Now I wear a girdle and eye shadow. Somebody told me that eye shadow makes all your other features incidental. I wear lots and lots of eye shadow.

Kieran put his hand over mine and wished me luck. Then he left. I got very drunk and went home with an older guy. We did it in his garage so as not to wake his mother.

+

So last week, over the phone, I told my father that I had HIV. Not because I thought he should know, or for his support. It was just something to say. Something that might make him pause before he went on again about his riding lawnmower.

"I've got HIV, eh?" I said.

"Huh. What's that?"

"The virus that causes AIDS."

"Oh. Yeah. Huh. How'd you get in that jackpot?"

"I don't know. The usual way."

"Well. Isn't that something."

"Yeah."

"You still got those skinny dogs?"

"No."

I thought that was the end of it. But my news must have made an impression on him, because he called Sheila and told her that I had AIDS. She called me yesterday. "Ron. Ron? Ron! How are you, my love?"

"I'm okay. How are you?"

"I'm good. Dad told me that you haven't been well." Sheila sounded like she was on speed. "Dad-told-me-that-you-haven't-been-well" – it was all one quick word, the way she said it.

"What?" I said. "Oh. No. I'm fine. You mean the HIV?"

"Yeah! Yeah-yeah-yeah. Dad said you're – you're living with AIDS."

"No. No. I'm just HIV-positive. I'm completely fine."

"And what about your – oh! You know what? This is craziness. I have to see you. Let me come over right now."

"Yeah! But I have company right now. So."

"That is so great. I'm glad you're not all alone. What about tomorrow? I'll pick you up for lunch. Are you still on the waterfront there?"

"No. I'm at the Margaret Laurence co-op. On Dalhousie."

"Oh. Is that an artists' co-op?"

"Kind of."

"That's so fun!"

+

I pick out a blousy T-shirt. I walk downstairs, check my mail, and then go outside to wait for Sheila. She drives up in a new yellow car. An ugly Nissan-some-thing, but new nonetheless.

She waves. I wave. I remember to walk toward her car.

She's a twig. Ninety-five pounds, tops. Her lithe, little bicep flexes on the gearshift. Her hair is rotten-tomato red. She's wearing a tiny, orange terrycloth tank top and matching shorts. "Don't you look hand-some!" she says.

"You look good too. You're so tiny."

"I know. I'm so busy. I never have me time. I just forget to eat."

"What are you – are you still acting?"

She lets out this long, fake laugh. The car swerves a little. "No! No. Didn't Dad tell you?"

"No. We don't really talk about anything. I'm surprised he told you about me."

"Hmm. I think he's a bit more forthcoming with me. But. Yeah. I'm a personal trainer now."

"Oh! Wow. That's great. Do you work out of a gym?"

"I do. Yes. But I also have established quite a client base. Including – do you know Jaclyn Smith?"

"Really? Wow. I didn't know she lived in Toronto."

"She doesn't. But her former housekeeper, Arlene, she now lives in Toronto and has a very successful custom-made jewelry business. I've helped her meet and exceed all of her fitness goals. My advanced Kegel exercises were so effective, she cancelled her vaginal rejuvenation surgery and actually complained that her vagina was *too* tight. I'm sure she was kidding. Although she does often look like she is in physical pain."

I don't know where we're going. We run an amber light.

"Should you be telling me all this?" I say.

"Oh, she wouldn't care. She's an open book. She's great. She is a dear, dear, dear, dear, dear friend."

"I'm so happy for you," I say. "Do you enjoy it? The personal training?"

"I love it! It's freaky how much I love it. Sometimes I just catch myself and I'm like, 'do you have any idea of how fulfilled you are?' And I totally don't. Because I'm just so happy."

"That is so great. Where are we going?"

"It's - FUCK OFF!" She slams on the brakes.

"What is it?" I say.

"That asshole is following too close behind me! Umm. Tammy's."

"Tammy's?"

"The place I'm taking you. Is called Tammy's. It's on the Danforth. It's a - oh, what do you call it?"

"Restaurant?"

"No. It's like a café, but like they have in Europe? You know..."

"A pizzeria?"

"No! Shut up! What is the fucking word I'm trying to think of? Bee—"

"Bistro?"

"Bistro! Shit! Thank you! Bistro."

Red light. Sheila is rocking back and forth in her seat. "Ron. I've missed you so much. Are you sure you're okay?"

"Yes. Absolutely. I've been very lucky."

"Well. You look great."

"I do? Really? I've been feeling a little insecure."

We're in the right lane, about to turn right, when we're broadsided by a minivan. The Nissan is thrust up and over the curb and into a mailbox. We both buck to the side. I clutch my chest. Sheila is gasping and pounding her palms on the dash. "Oh my God," she says. "This is just perfect. Fuck me with a chainsaw! Fuck! Fuck! Fuck!"

"Are you alright?" I ask.

"Me? What about my fucking car? My fucking brand new Altima!" She kicks open her door. An elderly woman is slowly getting out of the other vehicle. She has a gash on her forehead.

"What the fuck are you doing, fuck face?" Sheila screams.

"I'm so sorry," the old woman says. "I don't know what happened."

"You fucked up my brand new car is what happened!"

"I have my chequebook with me," the lady says. "Let's go to the car, uh, repair and get an estimate. I'll write you a cheque."

By now I've gotten out of the car. I'm standing between Sheila and the old lady, whose blood is seeping from the forehead gash and is streaked across her brow zig-zaggy like New Wave makeup.

"Oh no-no-no-no-no," Sheila says. "You fucked up my new car, I'm going to fuck up your insurance premiums. We're doing this by the book."

"Please. I'm so sorry. I lost my husband recently. I'm 78 years old. I'd – please, I can write you a cheque for whatever it will cost. I don't feel so good."

Sheila does an odd, shivering pivot on one foot. "You are not hearing me! Look what you have done! To my car!"

The old woman starts to cry.

"Yeah, you'd better cry. I'm gonna fuck you up!" Sheila starts rehearsing with some air karate. A high kick. A left chop. I grab her hands and pull her to me.

"What is wrong with you?" I say. "Are you on drugs?"

"No, I'm not on drugs! I'm – my car is wrecked. And I'm standing up for myself. Drug use is not an issue here. Everybody does a little meth now and then. Everybody does a little meth. And I'm pissed off. I. Want. Justice!"

The old lady is starting to sway. The blood no longer looks like New Wave makeup; the blood – streaming down her face, staining her Peter Pan collar – looks like car-crash blood.

And so I do what a gallant man would do: I incautiously whip off my shirt, bunch it up, and press it to the woman's wound. The sun stings my clammy, bluish-white chest and back.

"Thank you, that's helping," says the old lady. "You're a nice man. How can one be so kind and the other one be so…"

"So *what?*" snaps my sister. "So righteous? So strong? Fuck. Once again, male privilege wins out, the dude takes his fucking shirt off and he's a big hero. But me? Fuck. Just mail me to Iraq and cut off my clit, why don't ya?"

"Okay," I say. "We've just had a little accident. Nobody's a hero, nobody's getting their clit cut off."

Sheila hyperventilates for a spell, then starts to sob in tandem with the old lady.

I'm mediating here. I never used to mediate. I used to exacerbate. I used to tell one writer friend that another writer friend thought that the work of the first writer friend was puerile and uninspired, and then tell the second writer friend that the first writer friend said essentially the same thing about the second writer friend's work, even if nothing of the sort was said. All so I could watch them ignore each other aggressively at the next wine-and-cheese thing.

Now I am a man with his shirt off. Even before I was deformed, back when my body was empirically beautiful, I never took off my shirt in public, except for that one time I did GHB at the White Party in Miami. But right now, I am an oddly shaped, shirtless man with his sickly stick arms around two tearful women, northeast corner of Pape and Gerrard. I hold them close and whisper reassurance, the stuff a straight man would offer his panicked girlfriend. " 'S okay, baby. We're all okay. We're so chill."

I kind of like this new, provisional persona. I will play it for all it's worth – beer-gutted, splay-legged, gruff, certain, burpy – at least until the ambulance arrives, when I will likely drape myself in an emergency blanket. Unless one of my "girls" needs the blanket more, of course.

DO YOU WANT TO BURN TO DEATH AND LOOK LIKE STEAK WITH HAIR?

About me: Welcome to my sobriety blog! My name is Helene Savant. I have lived in Winnipeg all my life. I am a recovering addict and breast cancer survivor. I have been sober since May 2009, and cancer-free since August 2008!

I love to write, so I started this blog in the hopes that my story – my ongoing, thrilling story – will be of inspiration to other people living (!) with illness and addiction issues. There IS life – thrilling, thrilling L-I-F-E! – after drugs and alcohol and, in my case, real breasts. Read on!

February 28, 2010

A bad day. Not the worst day I've ever had, but a bad, bleak one nonetheless. I considered all my little diversionary mental tricks, my little Helene bits of business – cardio, shopping, online chat, masturbation – and nothing appealed to me. I think I am simply going to sit in my plush, comfy pink chair in the living room, motionless. This goes against my basic nature, which is GO! GO! GO! 24/7, but I need to try a new tactic. My old tactics aren't working.

I think I might call a friend. Ekaterina is really my only fleshly, real-life friend. I don't normally reach out to fleshly, real-life friends unless I'm about to mount them or kick their sorry ass in racquetball. Maybe I will call Ekaterina, just to talk. About Jack. About what Ekaterina does to help herself during difficult times.

February 27, 2010

Tonight, at the tail end of a lovely meal at Red Lobster, Jack told me that he finds me "vexing and exhausting," and he doesn't want to see me anymore, in any capacity, ever! I was blindsided. I asked him why he hadn't, at the very least, delivered the news before we had dinner. He said he was hungry.

I am despondent. If I wasn't so strong in my sobriety, I would relapse right now. Since coming home, I have cleaned the bathroom and pleasured myself twice. One day, one moment at a time.

I just don't understand. Things were going so well.

February 26, 2010

Dawn. Jack just left, the end of perhaps the most perfect date in the history of romance. My life is wondrous! There are dark, glittering, lilied troves here and there, everywhere, in my wondrous life.

We met up at 3pm, played racquetball for two hours (I kicked his sorry ass – yessssss!), then I sat with him while he lay down on a courtside bench (he felt faint). While he recovered, I talked about my journey over (*OVER*, not *through*!) cancer and opiate addiction. I talked and talked; remembering that we had first met on a smoking cessation message board (even though I don't smoke and never have), I made sure to make up details about my journey over tobacco, too.

After that, we showered (separately! Ha ha!) and went to dinner at this vibrant new Mexican restaurant Screamies. All the food was incredibly spicy; Jack and I stared at each other, panting and fanning ourselves like two Sahara vagabonds on their last legs. So yummy.

After that, we went to see that new action film (I'm terrible with movie names) starring that blonde actress (I'm worse with movie stars' names!), the movie in which the blonde actress has to dig her way out of the centre of the earth with a spoon (or something along those lines; I wasn't watching the film, I was watching Jack!).

I looked at his face in the darkened theatre and thought: I could abide with this man. I could rest with him. We could sleep so sweetly together. I would pare his toenails if he asked me, I thought to myself.

After that we went back to my place, Jack took a Viagra, I climbed aboard and rode him all night. I rode and rode and rode and rode. Once or twice he mentioned that he was tired and sore, but we all know what that means!!! I kept right on riding! I climaxed twice! I think he came, too. I couldn't really tell; he's such a suave, discreet lover.

And he was completely unfazed by my reconstructed breasts. He fondly fondled them. So unlike my ex-husband, as you will recall if you've been reading my blog from its inception.

My ex-husband was initially very supportive when I was diagnosed, constantly reassuring me that he would always find me beautiful and desirable. But my implants frightened him. He'd accidentally brush against them in bed and shudder, as if my new boobs were electrical or something. Fuck him. I delight in the knowledge that he is languishing at the very bottom of the food chain in prison.

Back to Jack. During afterglow, I nuzzled against him and asked him to sleep over; he said he was "too tired." Too tired to sleep over! I love dry wit. No "wet wit" for me!

Sobriety ROCKS.

February 25, 2010

My blog is being followed by three people now! After only nine months of blogging! I am going to put on my joggers and jog to Winners and buy whatever the hell I want! I've earned it!

February 24, 2010

I love my sister, but talk about a stick in the mud! As you know, she came down last week to support me during the trial. I wanted to do fun things, to celebrate my ex-husband's incarceration and inevitable, repeated ass rape. I wanted to play paintball, go to the casino, the racetrack. I did NOT want to go to Mass and wring my hands and talk about my feelings and wonder aloud how it is that a loving God can allow a middle-aged man to blow a thirteen-year-old boy.

This was the first time I'd seen Judy since getting sober and I have to say, she's not how I remember her. She used to be a real good-time girl, full of one-liners, given to giddy gossip. She has always been devoutly Catholic, but she never has rammed it down my throat the way she did this visit.

"Oh," she kept saying, "you must feel forsaken, because of all you've been through."

"No," I kept saying, "I don't feel forsaken. I feel formidable." She just refused to believe that I wasn't angry at God. O, *she* of little faith, is what I say.

And she was *horrified* by my behaviour at the courthouse. Every day I wore my mean, ironic Macaulay Culkin T-shirt and sat as close to the front as I could get. I stood outside the courthouse, and I gave my two cents to the *Winnipeg Free Press.*

From today's paper!

PEDOPHILE CONVICTED

A local man was found guilty yesterday of sexually abusing a thirteen-year-old boy over the course of several months in 2008.

51-year-old Claude Savant was convicted of ten counts of forcible oral copulation, and three counts of lewd acts.

Savant did not show any reaction as the verdict was read.

Outside the courthouse, however, Savant's ex-wife was jubilant.

"I'm like a child at Christmas," a beaming Helene Savant declared. "This verdict is a victory for the ex-wives of pedophiles everywhere."

Thrilled as I was to have been quoted in the newspaper, I'm still miffed that the nitwit reporter left out the part where I said that the verdict was also a victory for the victims of pedophiles everywhere. The quote in the paper makes me sound so self-absorbed.

As Judy and I drove home from the courthouse yesterday, she said I'd handled myself "deplorably!" What the hell does she know about handling one-self in a crisis? So her stupid Springer Spaniel broke a leg last month – ooh, time to call in the prayer circle! I said as much and it really set her off: God this, Mary that. I told her I didn't want to hear it, that the very reason I avoid AA is all the higher power bull dung. I couldn't wait to drop her at the airport.

When I got home from the airport later that night, I literally ran to the computer to check in with my var-ious online support groups. I went into all the chat rooms, posted umpteen times, but nobody responded. Some people actually left the chat rooms as soon as I'd post.

I wasn't offended or hurt. I get it: sometimes other people's chaos is simply too much to cope with for the recovering addict.

I finally ended up in a Nic Anon chat room, for ex-smokers. I've never smoked, but I was desperate for contact.

I started a private chat with this man, Jack, who quit smoking New Year's Day. We sort of hit it off; he gave me the link to his eHarmony profile. He's seventy, a full twenty years older than I, but the grin he offers on all his eHarmony pictures hints at a playful sexuality. We've made a date for the 26th. I'm trying to not get my hopes up. How can I not, though? I'm ready for love again. Crazy, crazy love.

February 17, 2010

I'm sorry I haven't updated my blog for so long. I am perfectly well and strong in my sobriety, if anyone was worried. I've been mired in my ex-husband's trial (yes! It's finally begun!), and the last few details of my divorce settlement needed hammering out.

On that note, there might be another wee gap in my updates...because my sister Judy is coming for a visit! She's worried about me; she thinks I need "support." Ha ha ha! Ha ha ha ha! Oh well. Bless her heart. We're going to have so much fun. Judy's a crazy lady; we used to backcomb our hair into Bride of Frankenstein dos and then go out on the town to see who'd still bite! I haven't seen her since Christmas '06.

And Ekaterina called me! What a dear woman she is. Wanted to see how I was holding up through the trial. I told her that I'm flourishing, absolutely flourishing. Adversity hones and primes me.

Did I tell my "bottom story" already? I must have. Oh well, one can never revisit one's bottom story too frequently.

Summer 2008. I was finishing chemotherapy, finally. Home early from my next-to-last session, I walked in on my husband performing oral sex on a thirteen-year-old boy who was squatting on our ottoman. My mouth went into a perfect O. I slapped my palms to my face. I looked just like the boy in that movie...lemme google it...Macauley Culkin in *Home Alone*. My face stayed that way for days.

My doctor prescribed a nice sedative, Clonazepam, for my tattered nerves. At first I took it just before bed. But soon I was taking it more frequently. Several times the maximum dose. I popped those babies like Tic Tacs. My doctor is elderly and has asked me out several times while examining me; he had no compunction about renewing my prescription every week.

With Claude gone (I kicked his sorry ass out *pronto!*), the house felt somewhat empty. I got a cat from the Humane Society; I thought a nice, plump cat would infuse my lonely house with warmth. Ha! The fucking thing was more high-strung than I was! It used to balance itself atop my wrought iron headboard and then leap onto my face in the middle of the night, claws dug deep in my neck and forehead. So I brought it to Loblaws and set it loose when nobody was looking. I am an animal lover, and I am not proud of that move. Yeesh, addiction really warps you like a motherfucker, doesn't it?

I was still working at the library back then. Ekaterina is the head librarian and a long-time friend;

as my addiction worsened, she kept reducing my workload.

By spring of last year I'd been demoted from the desk and stacks; now I was Storytime Lady, reading once a week for a group of preschoolers.

One day in early May, I downed a handful of Clonaz right before storytime. Swooshy and mindless, I began to read aloud from *Hollywood Wives* by Jackie Collins. I got to a sexy part and – my shame blazes over this still – started pleasuring myself through my slacks. A little girl asked me why I was so itchy. Then I fell off my stool.

Ekaterina pulled me into the staff room. She said that the only reason why she wasn't going to fire me was because her sister had been an alcoholic, and she was the sweetest person in the world before she passed out drunk with a lit cigarette and burned to death. So Ekaterina gave me a last chance.

"Do you want to fall asleep and burn to death and look like steak with hair?" she said.

"No, I sure don't," I said.

She drove me home. She wanted me to go to the hospital; I refused.

After all, I've been on my own, doing things my way, ever since I left my alcoholic parental home at the age of seventeen.

Even when I was married, I was alone. Claude was always so ethereal, forever fading out of one room and into another. For years, I just thought he was gratuitously gentlemanly, maybe, *maybe* gay, absolute tops. I never caught even the faintest whiff of pederasty.

And so I kept house, and tried for children for fifteen years, night after night of dutiful, grueling *pound, pound, pound*, to no avail. I conceived once; I lost the baby three weeks in, bending over to pick up Claude's vintage hardcover copy of *Ricky Schroeder: In His Own Words*, which had fallen from the bookcase.

That was the end of that. Claude was slightly forlorn about my barrenness; mainly he was floaty and...not around.

Then, in 2007, breast cancer. Double mastectomy. A year of chemo. Sometimes Claude drove me, mostly I drove myself. When you're seriously ill, fending off fevers and frailty that could end your life at any time, and you sometimes lie in bed and listen to your own breathing, and your breathing sounds hard and exotic, a great, brass wing flapping, and you wonder: is this breathing new to me? Is this the prelude to a death rattle? When you lie with that fear and never once shake awake the man beside you for comfort...

Well, suffice it to say, I knew that I could and would quit stupid fucking Clonazepam by myself.

So, after Ekaterina drove me home that day, I sat myself down, and I said to myself, "You are a powerful, powerful woman. There is nothing that you cannot conquer. There is nothing that you are going to be enslaved to" – or "There is nothing to which you are going to be enslaved." I can't remember the exact syntax. I was drugged at the time.

It was rough – my hair went white – but I got off the damn pills. And then...I can't remember! I'm going to go back and look at what I wrote when I started the blog...

Ha! Here is what I wrote. May 30, 2009: "This is my blog. I am twelve days off the pills. Never again will I be subjugated. Never again will I kowtow. Goodbye, addiction! Goodbye, perverted husbands! Goodbye, breast cancer! I will be a furious blur from here on in. Constant motion: racquetball, and lots of sex, and the Macarena, and the Achy Breaky Dance, and the Hustle!

My real life starts now! SOCKO! POW!"

Wow. I was not lying! Was I?

Older entries >>

SHE WAS
A LITTLE TEAPOT

Mother's Day, and the two men and their mothers were all together for the first time. Lee had met Guy's mother Glenda, before, but Guy hadn't met Lee's mother Cheryl. She'd just been released from prison, end of April. Two years for driving drunk and backing into an old man.

But now they were all gathered in Guy and Lee's living room, eating Lee's lemon sponge cake, smiling, talking of the couple's lush lawn, and all the lawns that Guy and Lee and Cheryl and Glenda had ever known. Lee was convinced that he and Guy were growing apart. Guy felt as he always had about Lee: piqued, confused, lazily diagnostic, turned on. He knew that Lee was concerned about their relationship, but Guy wasn't concerned – apart from his concern about Lee's concern.

A little tornado was forming in the next township. Guy's crabapple trees were tilting in the wind. Glenda voiced concern for her collie at home, Wally, who tended to yip and shiver during storms.

"Oh!" said Cheryl. "You have a collie, Mrs. Hens-rud?"

"Yes. He's two. He's my life, since Guy's father passed. He loves to go golfing with me. Do you have a pet, Cheryl? Oh, and please call me Glenda."

Cheryl smiled and studied her bunioned bare feet. "I haven't had much of anything since the – time away," she said.

"Since the incarceration," Lee said.

"Yes, since the incarceration. But when Lee was little, we had a collie. Mel. He was a sweetheart."

"He was a biter," said Lee. "He bit my friend Lacey, and he bit me. In the buttock. I still have a big dent."

"You were teasing it," Cheryl said.

"How? With my buttock?"

"Please don't grill me. You know I'm foggy about that period. That's when I had my hysterectomy."

Guy stood. Clapped his hands together. "We have iced tea, Diet Coke, all sorts of booze. What can I get you?"

"I'll have my usual, hon," said Glenda.

"Could I possibly have a gin and tonic?" Cheryl asked.

"No, you could not," Lee said.

Guy took Lee by the arm. "Let's go see what we can whip up," Guy said, and guided Lee into the kitchen.

"You're being so hard on your mother."

"No, I'm not. She's practically a murderess. She shouldn't be drinking."

"She can have one little gin and tonic."

"Fine. You make her a drink, and I'll go find a person for her to run over."

In the living room, Glenda pretended that the boys couldn't be heard. "Cheryl, Guy tells me that you once owned a convenience store."

"Yes. For 20 years. That's where Lee grew up. He'd set up his Lego in an aisle and play. That was, yeah. I lost the store to my husband when he divorced me. When I was away, in prison."

"I can't imagine how difficult that must have been for you."

"It was very hard. I'm out now, but I feel like I'm still in there. I feel like they're going to drop by any minute and put me back in. Oh well. So, I bet you have a really nice house."

Guy returned with a scotch and soda for Glenda, and a gin and tonic for Cheryl.

"It's a sanctuary," Glenda said. "It was a sanctuary, I should say. I miss Guy's dad very much. He was so big and loud, in the best way. Now...well, it's a very big, old house. I feel like Miss Havisham. And the upkeep is simply *beyond*."

"But you have Jim looking after things," Guy said.

"Jim. Yes. He's a godsend. Although, the other day, he was doing something to the driveway, and as I walked past him, he said, 'It's not right to see you all alone. You're not meant to be alone in the world.' Can you imagine? My groundskeeper has been musing on my place in the world. What next? Is he going to offer to bathe me? If Guy's dad were alive, he would've felled him with one punch! Of course, if Guy's dad were alive, I wouldn't be alone in the world, so Jim wouldn't have made that statement."

Guy rolled his eyes. He didn't like his big, loud father. The qualities in his father – the bigness, the loudness – that made his mother feel cosseted and dainty only ever frightened him. And Jim the handyman – why pick on Jim? He had always been the philosophical type. He would never attempt to bathe Glenda.

A thunderclap. Cheryl twitched.

"You're like my Wally about bad weather," Glenda said. "If I scratch you on your fanny, maybe you'll settle too!"

"Oh, I don't like that kind of...I don't even have a fanny. Or do I? What is a fanny? Never mind, I don't want to know. I'm going to talk about something else. Do you have a maid, Mrs. – Glenda?"

"A maid! Do I come across like someone who'd call their housekeeper a maid? No, I don't have a maid at present. But I will definitely need some form of help around the house when I get my knees done in June."

"Well, I love housework. I find it so calming. I'd love to be your maid."

Glenda threw her head back and laughed. Guy grinned, but inwardly lamented his mother's glossy self-involvement. Lee nodded, slowly. He liked Glenda; he admired her mettle. Guy, he found annoying and flimsy, at least this afternoon.

"How solicitous of you, Cheryl," said Glenda. "Thank you. You're much too sophisticated to be a cleaning lady, but it's sweet of you to think of me."

"I mean it," Cheryl said. "I could really use the work. I'm going wacko in my apartment. Could I be your maid? Please?"

Lee looked at Guy, then at Glenda.

"Please ignore my mother," he said. "She's relentless. She won't stop until she's guilted you into getting what she wants."

"Lee," Guy said.

"*Guyyyyyyy!*" Lee said.

"Really, Lee, Cheryl. I'd like to address this topic. Just let me go the bathroom first."

Glenda went to the bathroom upstairs.

The rain began. Hard rain, drumming the awnings.

They listened for awhile.

Guy broke the spell with a clap of his hands. "It's completely understandable," Guy said, "that you would want to find a little job somewhere. One that isn't too stressful."

"Thank you," Cheryl said. "Thank you for your support. I've always liked you. I've always thought that if Lee insists on being a gay, I'm glad he's hooked up with someone nice and hygienic. His last one was always going on about the earring he had that was halfway between his wang and his asshole."

"Don't opine on my relationship," Lee said. "You're such an infant. 'Please let me be your maid.' Shit. Clean your own house first."

"You're so mean," Cheryl whined.

"You are being very cruel," Guy said.

"Stop being so serene, Guy. It's really fake."

Glenda returned. She'd pulled her silver hair into a ponytail.

"What I want to say," Glenda began. "I know now what I want to say. Cheryl, I'm looking forward to a long and nourishing relationship with you, mother-in-law to mother-in-law. I'm so, so thrilled by that prospect. I wouldn't want to muck about with our friendship by any sort of professional entanglement. And, given that I'm on the town council and I'm active in my church, obviously I couldn't have a – someone who..."

"A convict," Lee offered.

"Well, yes. I couldn't have a convict as my housekeeper. And the wife of the man you injured goes to my church. Hey! Maybe you should do some sort of volunteer work with, umm, oh...what is the name of that disease that Ann-Margret's husband has?"

Sheet lightning.

Cheryl stood. "Okay. Got it. Message received. I'm not allowed to be alive. I had an accident and now I should just be chopped up and fed to the pigs. Well. Fine. You don't know. I am a lonely person. I used to be a store owner. Do you know what a Chinese lesbian made me do in jail? She made me wear this stinky blonde wig, and she made me sing 'I'm a Little Teapot' and act it out and everything. Whenever she wanted. Or else she said she'd sit on my face in the night. Do you know what that's like?"

Glenda opened her mouth to say something conciliatory. But Cheryl was crying now, crying and screaming, and could not be stopped.

"I'M A LITTLE TEAPOT! SHORT AND STOUT! HERE IS MY HANDLE! HERE IS MY SPOUT! WHEN I GET ALL STEAMED UP! HEAR ME SHOUT! JUST TIP ME OVER! AND POUR ME OUT!"

Lee stood and tried to embrace his screaming mother. She pushed him away.

"I'M A CLEVER TEAPOT! YES, IT'S TRUE! HERE'S—"

Glenda got up and pinched Cheryl hard on her upper arm. "Cheryl," she barked, "stop this now! We've all had hard times. I was accidentally shot at in Costa Rica in '94. We all have a bit of post-traumatic stress disorder. We can't go around screaming nursery rhymes like we're in some Romanian orphanage. My goodness. How on earth did you ever manage to raise a child and run a store?"

"She didn't!" Lee said. "She didn't manage. The store is long gone and, well, look how fucked up I turned out to be!"

Glenda shook her head, her onyx infinity symbol earrings swinging to and fro. "God! Why is everyone being so shrill? I really can't bear it."

"I thought you liked loud people," Guy said.

"There is a vast, vast difference between *loud* and *shrill*, my son. You of all people should know that – you've travelled throughout Europe. God, I need a Capri."

"I'll come with you," Guy offered.

"No, don't. Okay, do. But please don't speak. Please just be silent while I smoke my Capri."

Glenda walked out of the room, rooting around in her purse for cigarettes. Guy followed her.

Cheryl sank onto the ottoman, wiped her nose on her sleeve. "Jeez," she said, "she's a real snooty thing. Some people you just can't act natural around. Capris, tsk. You can always judge a person by what brand they smoke. When I saw your dad smoked Rothmans, I should've run for the hills!"

Lee was about to tell his mother to shut the fuck up, but as he watched Guy and Glenda out on the patio, through the sliding glass doors – Glenda languidly smoking her Capri, Guy smoking not at all, having swapped smoking for yoga many months before – and he thought of the pack of his beloved Belmonts in his shirt pocket, he wondered if maybe his mother might be well and truly onto something.

SCOODLY! DOO!
WOP! WOW!

When I first started out, I had at least three octaves.
Three-and-a-half, if I was good and warmed up. It was
a freakish, gaudy instrument, my voice. And I was
shameless with it. Forever lapsing into R&B vocal
runs, brandishing my great legato. I opened for Rita
Coolidge, the first half of her '81 tour. Whenever she
took the stage, she'd always praise me and worry
aloud that she wouldn't be able to top me. Rita's a
wonderful lady. She knows all about acupuncture
and has a gorgeous collection of vintage pewter earrings.

I should've taken care of my voice. As with any
other body part, I just assumed that it was always
going to be there. So I smoked three packs a day and
drank and stayed up for days at a time. Now, at 54, my
voice is shot. I have the range of a dial tone. I have to
talk-sing my way through most songs now, or set the
key so low that the song is often unrecognizable.
Where once I would've held a high note with a tight
vibrato, now I've been reduced to exclaiming "Hey!" or

"Whoa!" at the end of a tune. It's a miracle I still get gigs. Not that I get many.

If it wasn't for the money my first husband left me when he died, the divorce settlement my second husband was forced to fork over when he left me for that wanky "movement artist" bitch, and the royalties I get for writing the two Canadian hits I wrote back in the '70s, "Cats and Dogs" and "Easy Green," I'd be eating cat food in a gutter. As it is, I have a nice little condo in an ugly part of town. My friends' artwork adorns the walls. I have an elderly pug named Hettie and two cats, Vlad and Farrah.

I once read (I think it was in *Elle* or *Vogue*) that it's better to have two or three designer outfits that you wear over and over until they're in tatters than to have lots and lots of cheap clothes. I have three Issey Miyake dresses. Highly structured, layered things in various shades of grey. They hide all my figure flaws. They cost a fortune. I actually had an anxiety attack buying the last one, and the girl had to bring me some water. But I wear the dresses almost every day, even to the grocery store. Once, when I was at the pharmacy picking up my estrogen suppositories, a little boy looked me up and down and asked me if I was a vampire.

It would figure, the one night I don't wear my Issey for my weekly gig at the Carafe, the night I wear some shitty old pantsuit with a coffee stain on the ass, is the night that Roy and Nina would come to see me. They must've thought I was really hard up.

The Carafe isn't my favourite gig, but I make a little pin money and the house band is a sweet bunch of guys. I do old crap like "September Song" and "For Once in My Life." And I let the boys have their fun and do a little jazzbo riffing. I hate jazzbo riffing, but what can you do? Occasionally I join in, half-heartedly. "Scoodly! doo! wop! wow!" and all that kind of bullshit. Yuck. It's living death, but you've got to let the boys kick it out sometimes.

The night that Roy and Nina came, a month ago, I closed the set with an old Leonard Cohen favourite of mine, "The Guests." It's easy to sing, kind of an incantation. A song like that redeems the evening for me, even if it makes the regulars tune right out.

I finished the song the way I like to finish a song – no jazzbo riffing when Wanda does Cohen – and there was tepid applause. Except for this skinny young couple right up front. They stood and hooted, clapping wildly. I haven't had such a passionate crowd response since I did *The Alan Thicke Show* in '83. It was almost embarrassing. I smiled and made an *aw, shucks* face.

They cornered me as soon as I stepped off the stage. They were wearing identical black-framed glasses. She had a fussy Louise Brooks pageboy. He was wearing a bolo tie that, ordinarily, I would find highly suspect, but he looked like an ironic kind of guy so I gave him the bennie of the doubt.

"You're were astounding," he said.

"Incendiary," she said.

"Riveting."

"A sorceress."

I smiled, speechless.

"I'm Roy Irwin. This is my wife."

"Nina Sanderson-Irwin. It's such a thrill to meet you!"

"Oh my goodness. Thank you. I'm Wanda."

"Oh, we know," Roy said. "We have all your records."

"All two of them? You *are* fans."

They pulled me to their table and offered to buy me a drink. I said that I didn't drink anymore, but I would have a Diet Coke. They looked at each other. Then Roy went to get me a soda.

"Roy has just been obsessed with you since he was a little boy," Nina said. "The first 45 he ever bought was *Easy Green* in '75. He was ten."

"Seventy-six."

"Seventy-six, sorry. He was eleven."

"An eleven-year-old boy is buying records about some chick's boyfriend woes? You sure he's not gay?"

"Ha! Not gay. Just discerning."

Roy arrived with my Diet Coke.

"Soooo," he said. "We came tonight because we have a little proposition for you."

"Hey. I haven't had a three-way since I was a brunette!"

Perfunctory laughter all around.

"We're filmmakers," Nina said. "Documentarians. We've done some good work. Won some awards. I don't know if you've heard of us."

"God, I don't know anything about anybody. I sleep a lot."

"We want to do a piece on you," Roy said. "Very much in the vein of the Chet Baker docu *Let's Get Lost*, or the Rodney Bingenheimer docu *Mayor of the Sunset Strip*. You've seen one or both of those, probably."

"No. I don't tend to watch documentaries. My real life has been more than enough for me."

They looked at each other again.

"We're really excited about this prospective piece," Nina said. "We'll track you as you tumble from brief Canadian stardom to pop lore oblivion. The rise and fall of. Groping your way back to a state of grace. From the chrysalis of despair, the pupa of normalcy. That kind of thing."

"Interesting. I only wish my life were that interesting. I mainly just watch CNN and brush my cats."

"Not to worry," Roy said. "The narrative will emerge eventually. It's an alchemical process."

"Do I get paid?"

"No."

"Huh. Do I get to play any of my new stuff?"

"Absolutely. We insist."

"Okay. And how long would this take?"

Nina pondered the air. "How long did *The End of Frank Leafy* take, all in all, Roy?"

"A few months, absolute tops."

"Oh," I said. "I think I saw that one! Is that where the guy has a rubber doll for a girlfriend and he wants to marry it?"

"No," they said in unison.

"Oh."

+

Next day, I called my boyfriend to tell him the news. Louis is a psychiatrist. Wrapping up his residency at the nuthouse at the bottom of my street. He's twenty-two years younger than me. I'm always telling him that it'll never work out between us, that it's transitory, and I'll be left old, alone and ravaged. But then we keep on having fun.

"What'll they do when they find out I'm boring?"

"You're not boring. I think it's a fantastic idea. It'll be kind of like – have you seen—"

"Don't ask me if I've seen some documentary because I haven't seen any. Except for the one where the guy has a rubber doll for a girlfriend. And the one with Madonna where's she's wearing the cone bra."

"I hope they won't force me to be in it."

"Of course they will. My young boyfriend of colour? Old, ravaged white on young, sleek black? Interracial *and* intergenerational love? It's the only vaguely titillating thing I've got going on."

"Well, I'm very proud of you."

"For what? Being washed up?"

His doctor beeper thing went off and he had to go. I cut my toenails and watched *Judge Judy*.

+

"Okay, Wanda! Try walking a bit more slowly. And try to look – sort of distracted and anxious. Like you're waiting for biopsy results. That's good."

I'm walking slowly, anxiously, through High Park. Nina's holding the camera. Roy is barking orders at me. I always thought that documentarians weren't allowed to direct the action or mould the mood of the subject. But I guess I'm mistaken, because Roy has been bitching at me all morning to look subdued, look haunted, look sexy yet shy, look – no joke – "vaguely tuberculoid." It's been quite draining. I'm not Jessica Lange.

My friend's husband jogs past me, and I smile and wave. Roy yells "cut." Nina rolls her eyes, excuses herself and drags Roy behind a tree. She draws back her hand like she's about to slap him, then stops. "This DOESN'T feel GOOD!" She screams certain words, gathers herself, loses herself again, resumes scream-ing. "This feels very familiar AND VERY BAD! I THOUGHT WE WERE GOING TO try it MY way this TIME! I THOUGHT WE WERE going to try to BE A LITTLE MORE ORGANIC!"

I can't hear what he's saying. He's taken off his glasses. He's trying to placate. They both pause, eyes cast downward, before returning to me.

"Okay," she says. "Let's just go and sit on that bench. I'm going to ask you about the early days."

We sit on the cold, wet bench and I give her an abridged version of how I got my start. Gary Mackie saw me live and signed me to his agency. We shopped around my demo for a year, and RCA finally took the bait. The first single was...God, what *was* the first sin-gle?

"Those lean years," Nina says. "They must have been filled with desperation and self-doubt."

"Sometimes. Mostly it was fun. I made good money waitressing, had lots of—"

"Sorry. Could you include my question in your answer? That would be really helpful."

"Oh. Sure. Umm. Those lean years must have been filled with desperation and self-doubt, but they weren't. They were mostly fun—"

"Sorry. Could you sort of integrate my question into your answer a little more so it sounds a little more authentic?"

"Umm. Okay. Umm. When I look back on the lean years, sure there were moments of desperation—"

"Such as?"

"Umm. I remember, at a bar one night, running out of smokes. I didn't have any money, so I stole a fiver from the bartender's tip jar. I am really not proud of that one. I'm still paying off the karmic debt. Otherwise, it was a lot of fun. A whole bunch of us used to—"

"That's great," Nina says. "We'll leave it for now. There's no heat in this topic. Let's find a topic with heat." She leafs through her loose-leaf notes. "Am I mistaken, or do you have hepatitis C?"

Roy does not look happy.

"Now who's the provocateur, Nina?"

"There's a difference between professional focus and acting like you're Stanley-fucking-Kubrick, you wanker," Nina says, still looking at me.

+

They tried to reach my estranged mother, but she hung up on them. Calls have been made to Anne Murray's management, and Gordon Lightfoot's, and Burton Cummings'. I've never met Gordon Lightfoot or Burton Cummings. I brushed past Anne Murray on our way to neighbouring stalls in the bathroom at the Juno awards, mid-'70s. She took a shit. I did a bit of blow. I doubt she'll remember me.

Louis is going to talk to them next week. He's so cool and restrained; I hope he offers up more than "yes" or "no."

We sat on my purple paisley couch for today's interview. Hettie was very barky, and she's never barky. I don't think she likes Roy and Nina. Last time she was this barky was when I brought home a guy who turned out to be a serial killer. We went out twice. Later, when he was exposed as the serial killer, I admit to being a little offended that he hadn't tried to kill me. Why didn't I fit the archetype? Was I too jaundiced even back then? Was the light in my eyes not bright enough for him to want to snuff it out?

That was a story I could've told them today. But Nina only wanted to focus on my *heyday.* She held the camera and asked the questions. Roy sat in the kitchen reading one of those snobby magazines, *Harper's* or *The New Yorker.*

"After your first big hit, you must've felt destined for international stardom."

"I thought I had a chance, sure. The record company went all out to try and break the single in the States. But it just died. One executive bonehead said that my Canadian accent – my hard *r* – was alienating to the international market."

"How did that failure make you feel? Did you want to die?"

"I don't know. I guess it was disappointing. But I was 22. The options seemed endless. Do you mind if I smoke?"

"No, please do. Actually, lemme get some stuff of you just smoking. Really suck on it."

She orbited me. I seized and almost forgot how to smoke.

"The lonely lady smoking in her modest apartment," said Roy, still reading. "Very innovative, Nina."

"Just being thorough, Roy."

"Never work with your spouse," Roy warns me. "Negotiating a shared aesthetic...can feel like castration. Christ, we wouldn't even be married if it wasn't for Nina's hysterical pregnancy."

"It was not a hysterical pregnancy, you woman-hating cocksucker! I miscarried. You saw the discharge!"

Hettie got all barky again. Hettie wasn't happy. Vlad and Farrah were hiding. I stubbed out my ciggie.

"Guys, please. Enough with the sniping. Not in my home. It wrecks the vibe. I'll have to burn some sage or something."

"We're sorry," Nina said. "It's a bad patch. There is stasis occurring. We're trying to address it. Wanda, what's your biggest regret?"

"Smoking. I destroyed my voice. Suck-ups will say that my voice is sultry and jazzy now, but I hate sultry and jazzy. So – smoking. And maybe not having a baby."

Roy looked up from his snobby magazine.

"You really want to be a mother," he said.

"Hmm. Not really. I'm an artist. I'd love the baby to bits for the first month, then it would bug me. And I can't stand school-age children. I refuse to babysit my friends' kids. So – forget having a baby. I only regret smoking."

With that, I light up another. Thought it would make for a nice movie moment. I'm almost starting to enjoy the documentary process.

+

There's not going to be a documentary after all. And thank God for that. I've never been so demeaned. And by such total wackos!

They came to my place again today. Nina's hair looked greasy. Roy was obviously hopped up on something, and not just coffee. The way his knee joggled – he would've given a toddler whiplash.

He started right in with booze questions.

"When your American breakthrough didn't happen – is that when you became an alcoholic?"

"No, no. I didn't start in heavy duty with the booze 'til '82, '83."

"What was the catalyst? Your empty womb?"

Nina rolled her eyes and sort of snorted.

"No. There was no catalyst. I'd always been a social drinker. It slowly took hold. I kept a bar fridge beside my bed so I could have a beer before I got up."

"How bad did it get? Did you want to die?"

"No. I was raised Catholic. I'd never do suicide. It got pretty bad, though. I got fat. Blackouts, missed gigs, drunken gigs. It was actually my band at the time that did the intervention. And I didn't protest at all. I've got good horse sense, thank Christ. I've been sober since June 1986. 21 years."

I'm always taken aback when I say how long I've been sober. I'm not in AA. I don't do the "one day at a time" thing. I do the "smoke a lot of pot and eat whatever the hell I want to eat, in huge quantities" thing.

"Well done," Roy said. "Have you ever had a relapse?"

"No."

"Really? Not even one? Not even a little sip?"

"No."

"Do you crave it?"

"Occasionally."

Nina started whistling the *1812 Overture*.

"Let's try something," Roy said. "Let's have you drink some apple juice out of a champagne glass."

"Why?"

"It'll be an enigmatic moment. People will wonder if you've fallen off the wagon. Has she or hasn't she? It'll be a pivot point in the film. It'll be especially helpful if you can look sad and defeated as you drink the apple juice. Maybe throw in a little hand tremor."

"Absolutely not. That is beyond ridiculous."

Nina stopped whistling. She grabbed Roy by the hair.

"Your misogyny is boundless, isn't it? It's a miracle I haven't been assassinated!"

"Nina—"

Nina ran to my bathroom, slammed and locked the door.

"It really can't get any worse," she sobbed through the door. "I married my art therapist, and now I'm a zombie. I'm the living dead. All is lost. All is lost."

I asked Roy if I should call 911. He waved me away, started talking softly to Nina, his face pressed to the door. He called her "Nee-Nee" and kept repeating what a good, pure spirit she was.

I hadn't seen anything like it since the time I met Stevie Nicks backstage at a stop on her '83 tour. She was holding a heavily blanketed baby in her arms. I introduced myself. She introduced herself and then said, "Let me introduce my daughter, Simone." She parted the blankets to reveal Simone, who was an embroidered pillow. No joke. And Stevie wasn't joking either. She really seemed to love her daughter, the pillow.

Finally, after maybe ten minutes of Roy's cooing and baby talk, Nina came out, unharmed.

"I just want to have a healthy relationship that is at once peaceful and stimulating," Nina said, unable to make eye contact.

"We have that," Roy said.

"No, we don't. We have an anxious and stultifying relationship. 'Member two mornings ago, when you starting choking on porridge and I just sat there, pointing and laughing? If our marriage was healthy I would've given you the Heimlich, if I knew the Heimlich."

"Well, I forgive you."

"Ugh, I don't want you to forgive me, I want love. Sturdy love. Look at Wanda – she copes daily with addiction and failure, and she still has a successful boyfriend of colour. Wanda, how do you – what should we – what do you think we should do?"

Once, backstage in Vancouver in the '80s, a speeding, bleach-blonde girl with a perfect circle of purple rouge on each cheek asked me if I thought guys really care whether "the carpet matches the drapes" or not. I didn't know what to say. In many ways, I remain an innocent; I truly thought she was talking about upholstery.

Here in my kitchen, confronted with the pleading faces of these two banshees, wanting more than anything to smash their heads together for wrecking six weeks of my nice life, I nonetheless gathered myself and quickly scanned my entire romantic career for any tiny insight I could offer. And, for once, they waited, in respectful, expectant silence.

"If I were you," I said finally, "and I truly mean *if I were you*, and not me, given my quote-unquote *disease*, I would kick back, strip down to comfy undies, put on some CSNY, and start working my way through a 2-4. Get good 'n' wrecked, savour your beer bloat, shut the fuck up and just check each other out. Really leer, a good, long time. It'll work wonders, dollar-to-a-doughnut."

They both nodded, gravely assimilating my suggestion. I could see they were really considering, from all angles, the possibilities of drunkenness in their marriage. But before either of them could speak I felt this scream swoosh up my body and out my mouth. I'm not a screamer, just like how Hettie's not a barker, yet here I was, screaming. Screaming, and pushing them out my front door.

So, in that moment, something good did come of my time with Roy and Nina. And that something was not introducing two tight-asses to the curative power of booze.

The good thing was: when I screamed suddenly, I hit a high C, a note I haven't hit in twenty years. And later, in the bathroom, I ran through "Easy Green" in its original key, effortlessly.

I don't know where it came from, my top end, or if it's back to stay, but I can't wait to try out some oldies with the boys this weekend. A whole oeuvre is available to me again.

Maybe, this weekend, I'll try some early, soprano Joni: "Ladies of the Canyon," "Night in the City." Or even (do I dare?) Minnie Riperton!

I'm so – God help me – jazzed.

ELLIPSES

Doug's new girlfriend looks a little like a walrus. Her name is Crystal. She's sitting on our couch next to Doug. Crystal has a tiny head, thin yellow hair, a wrinkly neck and a great big body. She's wearing a University of Manitoba sweatshirt, jean skirt and brown pantyhose. She is telling me that she was going to be a nurse but decided to be a stockbroker instead, that her current job as a parking lot attendant is a temporary thing. As if I care.

Mom, who has been in the kitchen making vitality juice in the blender, comes out with a tray of drinks.

"Crystal," Mom says, "try my vitality juice. It's my little secret – if you've been wondering how I stay so young-looking."

"Okay. I haven't really been wondering that, though," Crystal says.

Not mean, Crystal. Just dumb.

"Oh!" Mom says. "A war of wits is going on here! I've got to be on my toes around this one."

"What does she mean," Crystal asks Doug.

"She's just joking around," Doug says. He takes a sip of his drink.

Without even tasting Mom's vitality juice, Crystal sets her glass down on the coffee table beside a coaster. Mom guzzles her drink. I don't usually drink Mom's vitality drink. But this time I do. I don't like Crystal.

"Are your parents in the area?" Mom asks Crystal. Mom's pink pedicure glistens in the sun.

"My mom is in Winnipeg, yeah. I'm estranged from my father, though. I'm not sure where he lives."

Mom rotates an earring, nods. "I'm sorry to hear that."

"Don't be. We don't like him. My mother said that he was filthy and uncircumcised, and the stink of his smegma made her eyes water."

"Oh. I've waffled on the circumcision issue. We had Doug done, but when I had Nelson here, I couldn't bring myself to mangle his genitalia."

"I'm not mangled," Doug says.

"You do sort of have that hanging flap bit on your dick," Crystal says.

"I so don't need to know that," I say.

Mom glares at me.

"Nelson! Don't be so regressive. We talk openly about anatomy and sexuality in this household. Vagina! Testicles! Anus! Cunnilingus!" She turns back to Crystal. "I'm sorry that Nelson interrupted you, Crystal. He really does know better. I've hammered it home. As a single parent, I've had to paint my parenting in broad brushstrokes – Nelson's table manners may be less than continental, for example, but he certainly knows that sexuality is always great conversational fodder. You see what I'm saying."

Before Crystal gets to say that she doesn't see what Mom is saying, Mom continues.

"There are twenty-five years between Doug and Nelson, and I really marvel at how very, very different they are. Nelson is so sophisticated, empathetic, courageous. And Doug is just great, but maybe a little bit...well, not *mousey*, exactly. I'm so happy that he's found such a strong woman."

"Yeah," Crystal says. "I am a pretty strong woman."

"I know you are," Mom says.

"I carried my wide-screen TV up three flights of stairs and wasn't even winded."

"Case in point. Well done."

There's a lull. I look at Doug. He is mousey. We don't look alike at all. He's a redhead and his arms and legs are like twigs. I'm big and brown. I come from a Trinidadian sperm donor. Mom had me all on her own. Doug is from Mom's first marriage. His dad shot himself in the backyard when Doug was two. I'm glad I'm from a sperm donor. We're fine, Mom and me.

"Show Crystal your portfolio," I say to Mom.

I love Mom's portfolio. She's been a successful print model for thirty years. She did runway stuff in her twenties, but she has really only come into her own in the last few years. She's one of a handful who has actually been more successful as an older woman. There are billboards all over the country of Mom jumping in the air, clad in a tennis dress, brazenly bra-less, full of elation because she takes Total Cal calcium supplements.

"Yeah," says Crystal. "Doug said you were like a supermodel."

Mom smiles. Goes into the den for her portfolio.

"I was never a supermodel. I'm just an every-woman sort of girl. I've been very, very blessed. I've met Joan Rivers, John Denver..."

She wiggles between Doug and Crystal on the couch. Doug makes room. Crystal sort of leans away.

"Here I am in '68," Mom says. "This one was for some terrible cereal, if I can recall. I'd just met Doug's father. He was such a brilliant man. He loved James Joyce. Awful lover. Doug's father I mean. Not James Joyce."

"Turn the page," Doug says.

"This was my first Hudson's Bay thing. Look at those earrings. I was so young. I was all nerve endings. No coping skills. My goodness."

"Doug bought a patio set at the Bay for me," says Crystal. "Nice big umbrella. I can't sit in the sun. I get a third-degree burn in a few minutes. I'm so fair. Doug says my skin is like – what did you say my skin is like?"

"Yogurt."

"Yogurt!" Mom says. "That's a terrible comparison, Doug. Aren't you a poet? Yogurt."

"Don't say that's a terrible comparison," Crystal says. "I thought that was a nice compliment."

Doug shakes his twig arm to make his watch face fall on the palm side of his wrist.

"I'm sorry, Crystal. Oh! Here's probably the most fun I ever had on a shoot. Fresca, 1981. I did cocaine. All the boys on that one have since died of AIDS. Too sad. Too, too sad."

"I don't like gay people," Crystal says. "There's one at Super Cuts who always wants to give me a bob, 'cuz it'll provide the illusion of a jaw line. That's what he said. I almost punched his lights out. So. AIDS. Sometimes you've got to think that maybe it's a good thing."

Mom's lips are pursed. I remember the time that Grandma said that meditation is just a fancy name for laziness. Mom's lips disappeared altogether that time.

"Here," Doug says, turning the page. "You look really nice in this one."

Mom glances at the picture, then at Crystal.

"That one was a freebie for breast cancer research. Given your feelings about AIDS, I wonder what you might think about breast cancer, Crystal?"

"I think I don't want to get breast cancer," Crystal says, laughingly.

"Well," Doug says. "You looked just great in that one."

Mom stands. Paces. Peers through the lace drapes. Paces. Mom is very ethical. Her integrity is very showy. Sometimes you just want to tell her to get off it. But I love that my mother is made of moral fibre. I feel safe. I'm fifteen but sometimes I still sleep in Mom's bed. I get scared at night.

"I could be a plus-size model," Crystal says. "I've been approached."

"Approached by who?" Doug says, eyes wide.

"Approached by fuck off. Don't you think I'm pretty enough to be a model?"

"I don't know. Yeah. It's not a matter of 'pretty enough.'"

Mom disappears into the kitchen and returns with a fresh glass of vitality juice.

"Crystal," Mom says, "have you heard of Yves St. Laurent?"

"Of course. The racecar driver."

"No. Yves St. Laurent was and is one of the greatest fashion designers who has ever existed. I worked for him once, one halcyon year, 1974. I barely spoke to him, but he imparted so very much crucial aesthetic wisdom with just a mumble or wave of the hand. Do you know why you could never be a model?"

"Because she's too fat," I say.

"Don't call my girlfriend fat! She has shin splints and that thing where you get sad in the wintertime."

"S.A.D.," I say.

"Yes, it is sad. Very sad," Doug says.

Mom sets her drink down on the window ledge.

"Crystal, it's not that you're not pretty enough or too fat. When I walked for St. Laurent in his showroom, and he accepted me, he said 'Yes. *Ellipses.*' Of course, he said it in French. But a girlfriend who also walked for him was bilingual and translated for me. *Ellipses.* Do you see what I'm getting at? Via St. Laurent?"

"I don't know. Where's the bathroom?"

"One moment. What Monsieur St. Laurent was saying was that a model must exude the promise of *more to come.*"

"More of what?"

"That is incidental. What's key is the foggy promise of *more to come.* A thrilling addendum, if you will. And you don't have that. As of yet."

Crystal looks at Mom like Mom has just keyed Crystal's corvette.

"You don't know what I have. I have secrets that I've never told anyone. I had a twin that was stillborn. I've never told anyone that. Remember, I told you about that on our first date, about how I'd never told anyone about that, remember, Doug?"

"Modelling isn't about looks," Mom continues. "It's sacred. It's a sacred greeting to all of the women in the world. One is saying, to the women of the world, 'Hi there, women of the world. Go forth and *seek your ellipses.*'"

"'Kay. Will do."

Mom looks exhausted. The Yves St. Laurent story always takes a lot out of her. Sometimes I think she feels bad that she chose commercial work and family, and didn't stay in couture and become a coke addict with an eating disorder.

"I'm sorry," she says. "I'm suddenly very tired. I need to lie down for a spell. Could someone start the vegetables? I'll be back in half an hour."

She weaves her way out of the room.

Crystal's yogurt skin is blood red. Doug looks afraid. I bet she'll beat him up on the bus home.

"What's wrong with your mother?" Crystal says to me.

"Nothing is wrong with her," I say. "It's called, 'having a personality.' You could learn a lot from her."

"Who's going to start the vegetables?" Doug asks, the mousey peacemaker. "You know I'm hopeless with that kind of thing, Nelson."

I look at Crystal. She looks at me. It's a stare-down. But with her tiny eyes and albino lashes, I can't really tell if she's blinking.

"Fine," she says. "Shit. I'll start the stupid fucking vegetables. Don't ever say that I'm not helpful and gracious. And, also, do not ever say that I don't have *ellipses* or whatever. I have *ellipses*. I have a lot of *ellipses*, Doug."

"I know you do, Crystal."

She struggles to her feet and goes in the kitchen. I hope she has learned something, anything, from my mother.

Doug and I sit as we've sat so many times before, staring into our laps, listening to the sounds of a cranky girlfriend banging about in the kitchen and faintly, far away, my vulnerable mother's small, enchanting, mysterious snore.

Jeanette, the Heretical Homemaker

April 6

I have to admit: once the kids were fed and off to school, and Max had left for work, I went back to bed.

Leo and me, we made love all night. In between, we'd lie there and stare at each other, telling little stories from childhood, listening to old Fleetwood Mac records.

I snuck in at five in the morning. Max woke up when I got into bed. I told him I'd been in the rec room all night, praying. He went back to sleep. I got maybe ninety minutes before the troops started trickling downstairs.

As the mother of four children, all of whom have Down's syndrome, I am often asked how it is that I cope with such domestic stress. I always say that having four children with Down's syndrome is not stressful – it's a wonderful blessing. That's what I always say. And usually I mean it.

Dodie is four. Rutger is seven. Simone is eight. And my eldest, my little man Fyodor, he's going to be eleven in May!

I love my family, my little team. I love them so much. I can't stand to be away from them for even an hour. They can be grueling, but in a gratifying way.

My husband took them to Fun Mountain last week. I had to have minor surgery. A benign cyst on my forehead that parted my hair. Dr. Fleur used a local anesthetic and cut it off.

I was fine during the procedure, but afterwards I got a little weepy. I wasn't myself. I tugged at Dr. Fleur's sleeve. It must have been the anesthetic. I'm told that I repeatedly asked Dr. Fleur if he was my daddy. And when Dr. Fleur said that he was not my daddy, I cried even harder.

"I'm so little," I'm told I said. "How long have I been a little girl?"

"Thirty-six years," Dr. Fleur supposedly said soothingly.

Then I came to my senses, and I was good to go. I'm so healthy, it's not funny. I'm like an ox. I'm like a thunderbolt. Or a tuba. I guess a tuba isn't a good comparison. You don't immediately think of physical strength when you think of a tuba. I'm like an ox. We'll leave it at that.

Max, my husband of seventeen years, was robbed at gunpoint, after a Midnight-Madness sale at the

Brick, Christmas-time last year. Shortly thereafter, he became born again as an evangelical Christian. He went away to some country church retreat for two weeks, he put on a woman's nightgown, and the congregation dunked him in an icy lake, by way of baptism.

Max has been just radiant ever since. So calm. He's stopped screaming in bad traffic. He shovels neighbours' driveways. Most of his shoes these days are slip-ons.

I've become born again too, sort of. I was baptized at Grainard Evangelical Hall along with all our kids. We go to church, and bake sales, and prayer meetings, throughout the year.

The whole family prays several times a day. Additionally, Max and I pray before bedtime. This bedtime prayer can sometimes go on for upwards of forty-five minutes. Max often weeps freely as he prays for the safekeeping of the American troops in the Middle East, and for the torment and downfall of homosexuals and every woman who has ever had, or has even considered having, an abortion.

Sometimes I chime in with the odd "amen" or "woo hoo!" but mostly I think about what we should have for dinner the next day. Or Leo. Sometimes I think about Timothy Dalton brushing the hair off my neck with his massive hand.

Max is happy for the first time ever, really. So I go along with it. The church scene can be tedious, but most of the people are really very nice. And the kids love it when everyone starts speaking in tongues. They think it's a game show.

The thing that sustains me – apart from my little team and Max and the religious faith crapola – is Leo. He was Fyodor's teacher, and now he's Simone's. We've always flirted. He's a wonderful teacher. So patient. His eyes blaze like neon. And his voice is husky, like my Uncle Garth's was when he was diagnosed with throat cancer. But Leo doesn't have cancer. Far from it. He's so strong. The two of us, oxes. Oxen, I guess I should say.

It was a few days after Max left for his country church retreat that I first called Leo. Very little was said. Pleasantries, then I asked him if he was busy. He told me to come over. I got my sister Frida to babysit. She's on disability because of her back. But she runs a small business out of her home. Handmade dog booties. She rakes it in. I can guilt her into babysitting anytime.

Leo offered me a glass of white wine and a piece of homemade carrot cake. He said my name, with his husky voice: "Jeannette." I've always hated my name. Grocery store checkout girls are called Jeannette. But the way he said it, sort of whispery, made "Jeannette" sound like some sort of secret password for entry into a special, sexy section of heaven.

He performed oral sex on me.

Max has never done that. Max always looks at my bush like it's a carpet stain or something.

But Leo went down on me, and he did it with gusto. Then he came up, his face just inches from mine. "I want you to taste yourself," he said.

Had it been Max, or anyone other than Leo, I would've either laughed or thrown up. But I let Leo kiss me. And I tasted good. A bit like a nice roast.

We made love every night for eight nights. At first, I told Frida that there was a round-the-clock prayer vigil at the hospital for our minister's comatose little girl. Frida bought it initially.

But by day six, I had to come clean. Frida was elated when she learned of the affair. She's never liked Max. She told me to start divorce proceedings immediately. She said the kids would like Leo much better than Max, that I should even try to convince them that Max was dead or better, that he'd never existed. Of course, I would never do any of those things.

But I did let Leo put it in my ass. The pain was intense. But it was – cleansing. A healing pain. I don't know. I really didn't mind it.

When Max got home from the church retreat, he gave me a pussy willow, and went on and on about how he had been born again, that his perception of the world was now fresh and childlike because he was born again, that the reason the kids have Down's syndrome is so that they can live in a permanent state of being born again, and that if I didn't become born again we'd have big problems.

I became born again and met up with Leo whenever I could. Lunch hour. Middle of the night. He's just down the street. He has a nice little wartime bungalow. Hardwood floors. Red walls in the living room – red!

I am not in love with Leo. I realized that a few months in. He's too fair-minded, too measured; he is a masterful lover, but there is sometimes something a little too studied, too *Joy of Sex* about his technique. However, should he suddenly find his illogical, raging side, I would instantly and eternally fall in love with him. So there is that to look forward to.

Night before last, I was putting Dodie to bed and she asked me if we could get a dog. I said we'll see, and then I said that Daddy probably wouldn't like to have a dog around; It might go against something in the scriptures, or something like that. Then Dodie asked me if we could get a parrot. I said definitely not and who on earth would even want a parrot.

" Not me," Dodie said.

"Alrighty then," I said, and I turned on her Cinderella night-light.

+

April 7

When Max came home from work today, he told me that we're going to home-school the kids. He said he'd been mulling it over for a while. "The only way to buffer the kids from the heretical teachings of the public school system," he said, "is to teach them ourselves."

I laughed a little.

"But the kids aren't learning heretical things," I said. "They're learning life skills. They're learning how to open a combination lock, and how to write horizontally, and use paper clips."

"Please don't fight me on this, Jeannie. You know that heretical teachings can seep in, even with special ed."

He smelled like burnt rubber. I asked him if he'd recently rubbed against burnt rubber. He said he hadn't.

"And I suppose," I said, "that you want me to be the home-school teacher?"

"Yes. And I think you'll do a wonderful job."

"Please. Do you know how impossible it will be to instruct four high-strung children of different ages?"

"It will be fine."

"No. I refuse. I absolutely refuse."

He wiped away a phantom tear. Well, I shouldn't decisively say "phantom." It could've been a real tear; my astigmatism grows worse by the day.

"My heart is broken," he said. "I feel betrayed. I feel like you have betrayed me. I feel like you have betrayed the church. And the children."

"Don't speak for the church. The church doesn't care if I'm not able to home-teach four special-needs kids. The church doesn't care when I get my hair streaked. The church doesn't care that I like a nice, chunky, 3/4-inch high heel."

Fyodor came in the kitchen and asked what was wrong.

"We're fine," Max said. "You go away now, Fyo."

Fyo went away.

"If you don't home-school, you are spitting in the faces of our children. I – I may have to say prayers against you."

Max has two hunting rifles that he polishes several times a week. He could kill me and the children. I wouldn't put it past him. He is a zealot now. Actually, he may have been a zealot all along: for as long as I've known him, he's trimmed his pubic hair, balls and all.

At bedtime, we prayed together. I pretended to see the light. Max cried, definitely for real this time; I had my glasses on.

Once he was asleep, I called Leo.

"Leo," I said. "Oh Leo. Max is forcing me to home-school the children."

"Uh oh," he said.

"I know. What am I going to do?"

"Well," he said. "Do you want some help with your lesson plan?"

I wrung the dishcloth. I wrung and wrung it.

"I am just very frightened and overwhelmed. I feel so pinned. I can't breathe. It's like an enormous man is sitting on my chest. I'm scared. And stressed out," I say.

He asked me if I want to come over for some light Shiatsu. I say that someone's at the door and hang up.

Pen in hand. Pad on lap. By the light of an hour-long infomercial. I try my best to think of things that will meet everyone's needs, from Fyo down to Dodie.

Lesson Plan #1.

1. God created the universe.

2. A fetus is fully formed and aware at two weeks, so abortion is always murder.

3. Always wipe from front to back.

4. Don't argue with the police.

5. People of other faiths are all going to hell, unfortunately.

6. Multiple ear piercings make you look cheap.

No. Yuck! No! I know things. I do. I'm well read, for a high-school dropout. Camille Paglia, Joan Didion, the first four pages of *Remembrance of Things Past.* And I'm very astute about – how would you put it – social intangibles. How to stare down a man at a party until he propositions you. How to walk jauntily in heels on a midday sidewalk and draw admiring glances from men and women alike. Fail-safe ways of appearing sober when you're hammered. That kind of stuff. Occult life skills. A mother's true legacy.

7. *My lovely children, Down's syndrome is not a blessing, it does not place you closer to God, despite everything your father and I have told you. You've been shortchanged. You have. Given that: Do whatever the hell you want. Do what makes you happy. Do what feels good. If you want to rub up against a lamppost until you have an orgasm, do it! Don't worry about embarrassing me or Dad. Let it rip!*

8 a). You're a pedant and a buzz kill, Max. I fell for nice teeth, big, manly hands, a deep, lustrous speaking voice, masterful one-finger highway driving. Now I'm saddled with a simp. A gutless simp. Somebody startled you in a parking lot and you ran home crying to Jesus. Sex with you is as fun and mystical as a mammogram. The sight of your corned, curled baby toes every morning makes me want to pluck out my eyes with a butter knife.

8 b). Watch now as I turn your four children against you, day by day. I will fill their radiantly simple minds full of sinful notions. And damning facts about you. All the rancid jealousies that govern you. Your undescended testicle...oh, there is a wealth of material.

8 c). It's 5:15. You'll be awake in an hour and fifteen minutes. You'll pad downstairs, those disgusting baby toes sinking into our mossy-blue carpet.

I will still pour your coffee and your bowl of muesli. But when you ask us all to bow our heads to thank God for the muesli, I will not bow my head. I will not. You won't notice, of course, because your head will be bowed.

The kids will notice, though. They'll see my unbowed head bopping about, possibly making funny faces, and they will understand that this house is not the airless rectory you'd like it to be. This is a funhouse! A nuthouse! A flophouse! Drug addicts and people who like sex are welcome here! And that's just for starters!

+

His alarm goes off, loud and shrill as a fire drill. It's time for me to start his day for him.

Cloris for
one day

We're simple men. "We're simple men," is what we often say during dinner party lulls or three-ways that recede into conversation. And, in the main, we are simple. Simple, as in breezy, agreeable, moderate. We like the movies and music the masses like. We don't often read but when we do we read popular fantasy, we each buy a paperback copy and talk about it at bedtime. We read at exactly the same rate. There is unison everywhere in our lives. Our life.

It wasn't always this way. In our twenty years as a couple, one or both of us has been snipey, para-noid, depressive, given to operatic hissy fits, reduc-tive and cruel appraisals of character, booze, meth and poppers. There was some pretensions: Glen studied mime and "emotive movement" for two years; he found many, many ways of saying "I love you," wordlessly, during that period, most of which made me want to smash his face in. I was convinced for a couple of months six years ago that I was inter-gendered; I changed my name to "Oh" and demanded that friends and co-workers refer to me as "they/them," rather than "he/him" (eventually I realized that I was not intergendered, that I was really only a bit queeny). And until recently – last couple of years, really – I've not been above periodically accusing Glen of having an inclination towards misogyny so severe that, were he to witness a woman being boiled alive in a big cauldron, he'd spoon off some of the broth to taste. I've let that go, though. The long trek to total trust is bumpy and often confounding.

We clutched each other when we met, at the height of the epidemic, the two of us somehow virus-free, stilled by guilt. Our friends were dying, sometimes two or three a week, all of these beautiful men gone monstrous or ghostly, and so done in by getting out of bed they'd have to go back to bed.

We tended to them. We did our bit, day by day, and every night we'd cling to each other in bed, body heat being the only remedy for the day's horror.

We're all set now. We eat slowly, luxuriating in taste and texture. We've gone pot-bellied and slack-shouldered. We laze and nap.

We came through hard times toughened, but not jaundiced. I still pick dandelion bouquets and wedge them into empty salt shakers. I am a cook at a down-town place that chubby, jaunty, jet-black-haired young lesbians tend to haunt. Glen is a social worker. He manages to mete out compassion without going insane. I am very proud of him.

He had colon cancer eight years ago. He was 36. Came on quickly, caught early, treated – a five-foot length of intestine cut away but, thank God, no colostomy – went away and never came back. The whole episode was such an aberration, even with the chemo and the screaming red snake of a scar straight down the middle, where a line of luscious hair used to be, that we chalked it up to bad randomness and got on with things.

Glen wants to adopt. His mother died and we came into some money so we're thinking about buying a baby. Well, not *buying* a baby. Facilitating the private adoption of an unwanted baby, most likely from China or the Third World. Another gay couple with whom we play cards got a little girl from China. They named her Cloris. She's grown into a beautiful, stony, suspicious four-year-old. Who can say if she's innately that way, or if she's damaged by attachment disorder, or if she's simply bristling at the name Cloris. Anyway, our friends are happy, even if Cloris isn't.

I could go either way on the parenthood thing. I'm not dispassionate on the topic; if we have one, doubtless it will be a joyous experience and I will be transformed. If we don't have one, well, I already love our simple life. Mainly, I want Glen to be content. His contentment is all that I care about. I know that makes me sound like a doormat housewife, and I guess I am to some extent. When Glen is content, however, he is like antique light glinting about in a warm, wooden room. He is radiant. You can't help but be content when Glen is content.

We're dithering over what to do and how to do it. Surrogacy is too expensive, and we have ethical qualms about wrenching a child from its culture or immediate environs. Glen has ethical qualms, I should say. He knows all about attachment disorder; he once dated a black man who was adopted by a white family; the man felt so divorced from his authentic self that he talked like a robot and, during orgasm, could only muster a dismayed "oh," as if he'd just missed a lottery win by one digit.

There is a lot to think about. That's okay. We like to mull things over. We talk in bed, face to face on one pillow, sharing air, sometimes until morning. In this way, we'll decide what to do about a baby.

+

He calls me into the bathroom. The bowl full of blood. He looks up at me like a shamed child. This is how it went the last time. Bowls of blood. I was sure we were past all this. His illness was a curio, years ago. That's alright, I say, looking about for cleaning products, pretending that this harbinger is nothing more than a household mishap. I take the toilet brush and swirl it about in the bowl, reddening the brush's white bristles.

"What are we going to do?" he says.

I panic. I get panicky when he turns to me for comfort and counsel. There are so many possible approaches I could take that I can't pick one. I put my hand on the back of his now-damp neck. This could easily be hemmorhoids, I finally say. How many times have I had bad, bloody hemmorhoids. Gay man's burden. I'm sure that's all it is.

The endless batch of painful, tedious tests all over again. It's back, metastatic. I knew there would be rough patches in our quiet life, but this; we aren't prepared, we aren't set up for sickness like this. The house is too cluttered, our cats wander in off the street with vermin in their jaws, our curtains are diaphanous and let in too much light, I don't know CPR, I'm a terrible driver. And what about those nights, later on, as I sit in an office chair in the hallway, humming to myself to drown out the sound of his raspy breath? Glen is quite often the only evidence I can find of myself. Glen will die and our life, our lives, will end.

He wants to do the baby thing. He is suddenly resolute.

Our friends are agog.

His own meek mother has taken him in hand, emphasized, in a hard voice so unlike her that at first I thought there must be a hidden mic somewhere in the kitchen, that raising children is a "gut shredder" even for healthy people, that a sick person having a baby is tantamount to suicide.

But there is this new, rock-eyed, pummelling wilfulness in Glen; I was driving to Loblaws yesterday when he suddenly decided that he absolutely had to go to Metro instead. We were practically in the Loblaws parking lot. When I asked him to be reasonable and couldn't we get everything we needed at Loblaws, he started going "na-uh, nope, na-uh" like a six-year-old.

On the way to Metro I patted his thigh and told him that everything would be fine, Metro, here we come. Jesus, Jesus, he said out the window. Now was that so goddamn hard?

It is hard. Glen is unremittingly unlikeable. He may even be slightly demented. I feel insubstantial and bitchy for saying so. I want to be sturdy in this, but when you've come to understand a person as innately charming, even during arguments, hangovers, horrible holidays, how do you adjust and make room for them to be, at heart, an asshole? I've actually considered finding a support group, spouses-of-the-really-ill kind of thing, and then I think of the one that Glen and I went to, back in the AIDS day, a worried well group, and remember how all we did was nod and listen and study all the awful two-tone dye jobs and pleated, acid-wash denim. Why was it that our collective distress didn't manifest in our dress, those late '80s years? We should've been in the starkest widows' weeds. Nonetheless, it was fun to gab about it all afterward.

That's the thing: I'd go to a spouses-of-the-really-ill support group if my spouse could come with me.

+

"We're going to China like, tomorrow," he says. "They can't get rid of the girl babies fast enough. I've googled it. A girl baby will be, like, three grand, tops."

"Please, just take a breath, Glen."

"I don't want to take a fucking breath. You take a fucking breath, and hold it forever – how about that? I'm going to China to get a Chinese girl baby. You can come with me or you can stay here."

"Okay. I'll take care of the arrangements. Give me a few days. Please let me take care of the arrangements."

"Maybe I will, maybe I won't. You have twenty-four hours."

+

At the restaurant, some guy sends a steak back to the kitchen because the steak looks like pork. I want to smash the plate into pieces. Instead I look to Steph, the waitress.

"What the fuck? Meat is going to resemble other meat, always. Is he insane?"

She shrugs. Steph is such a stunned oaf at work. She's at least thirty, yet still so dreamy she takes her break in the bathroom where she can sing Disney classics in a mewling soprano. Her boyfriend is gorgeous, a bus driver. So maybe her home life is enchanted and she can't wait to step out of her uniform and get back to the enchantment – I don't care. If you can't share a strained laugh with the chef, fuck off and die.

In the alley behind the restaurant, I light up my first cigarette in six years. I call David, one of Cloris's fathers. He sounds congested. I tell him about Glen wanting to buy a baby. He gasps; his partner, Miles, was the guiding hand behind their adoption, and David has been exhausted ever since, one herpes lesion after another on his thin, bloodless lips.

"Christ, no," he says. "I adore Cloris, you know that, but she has run us both right into the ground. It's so hard. It's so not fun. If you had Cloris for one day, you'd wash your hands of the whole baby idea."

Naturally, I take him up on it. I ask him what day would be best to babysit Cloris.

"Any day," he says. "Tomorrow?"

+

Glen is driving, singing that horrible song in which the singer commands you to lick her pussy *and* her crack. He was up most of the night retching, post-chemo treatment, yet here he is, all chipper and excited to have Cloris for the day. His good moods are rare, so even though it's eight o'clock in the morning, my face is flushed from fatigue, and I despise the song he's singing, I try to bop along.

Cloris is sitting, prim as a schoolmarm, backpack in her lap, on the front steps of our friends' house. David watches from the front window, his little body bundled into a puffy black bathrobe. We gesture at each other: *Can we pop in for a minute? No, no, just go 'n' have fun, thumbs up!* Cloris stands silently, resigned to her day's fate.

She is hugged by Glen. I consider hugging her, then think better as I watch her shimmy her way out of Glen's arms.

"We're going to have so much fun, you'll never want to go home," Glen says. He goes to buckle her in; she's already buckled herself in. I sit in the back and look on as Glen prattles away to a silent, seemingly empty front seat.

"What do you want to do? Have you had breakfast, Clo?"

"I had Eggos. Two Eggos. And orange juice. My name is not Clo. It's Cloris."

"How about Clover?"

"How about Cloris? I don't want to be here any-more."

"I'm sorry, Cloris. Please don't be mad at me. I love you. You are a child of the light. I love you so much."

Glen has never spoken this way. Our conversa-tions about spirituality have always been digressive, spacious affairs, punctuated by a lot of shrugging and sighing. At no point has anyone uttered the words "child of the light," or even "thank Goddess," not even when Wicca was big back in '95. I sit more forward in my seat and put my hand on the armrest close to Cloris so she won't be as scared of Glen as she proba-bly is.

Cloris says all she wants to do is watch cartoons. Glen says that we can absolutely watch cartoons, but wouldn't she rather go to a park and muck about on the monkey bars?

"No way," says Cloris, "and what does *muck about* mean?"

"You know, to have fun and be crazy."

"Oh. No. I don't want that."

"No problem. No problem at all. We'll go home and get all cozy and watch cartoons, and it'll be just super."

Glen gets behind the wheel. His hand is trembling and the key can't find the ignition. He says he feels too fragile to drive. Jokingly he asks Cloris if she'd like to drive. Silence. I haul myself out of the backseat.

We swore off television years ago, put the set in the basement beside the dryer.

Now, back in his pyjamas, retching again, rifling through the cupboards for yummy things for Cloris to eat, he curses the day we abandoned TV. "What kind of snobby arseholes don't have a TV in the living room," he says between retches.

"We don't like television," I remind him.

"I HAVE NEVER SAID THAT I DON'T LIKE TELEVISION! Don't listen to him, Clo! Television is absolutely vital, in its own way. It binds us as a human family. I like television. I love television!"

I can't think of a response. I remember how, when our friend Lisa cancelled dinner plans so she could watch Oprah Winfrey's interview with Michael Jackson in '93, Glen pontificated for a good hour on the wasteland that was Lisa's inner life. I lit into him for his snobbery at the time; now I long for his snobbery. I long for precisely those dark qualities of his, those tics and lapses I used to gloss over or ignore.

I am making cinnamon toast for the three of us. I am doing this as slowly as possible so that Glen might conk out or Cloris run home screaming before I finish making cinnamon toast.

They are sitting on the deep freeze when I come downstairs with the plate. Cloris is watching TV, a cartoon featuring a talking lightning bolt. Glen is watching Cloris.

"I love this cartoon," Glen says to Cloris. "It's so fun. Is this your favourite cartoon?"

"No."

"Oh. No problem. What is your favourite car—"

"Please stop talking right now!"

Glen's strenuous glee fades fast. He is glum again. I remember Glen's glum. I've missed it. I'm glad it's back, if only for a moment.

The talking lightning bolt is angry about something and makes an electric sizzle sound.

Cloris likes the sizzle sound. She imitates it: "Szzzzzz Szzzzzz."

This is the happiest I've seen this little girl. I'll never forget the contempt with which she blew out the candles on her third birthday cake; this smiling sizzle sound is completely unexpected.

Glen leans against me. "She hates me," he says, muffled by my shirt sleeve. "She thinks I'm a bad person. Kids can tell. She can tell that I reek of death."

"Shut up," I say. "Szzzzzz," I go, like Cloris. "Szzzzzz."

"Cloris, Clo? Do you think I'm a bad person?"

There is space between Glen and Cloris on the freezer. I hop up, put my arm around Glen, put my other arm ever-so-tentatively around Cloris, with only my fingertips touching her tiny arm.

"Cloris," I say, sing-songy. "Szzzzzz. You like Glen, don't you?"

She sighs the sigh of an ancient charwoman at the end of a very long workday. "Don't you know," she says, "that it's not nice to talk when there's a show on. Everybody knows that. This is my worst day ever."

Her worst day ever. Well. That will not do.

I stand on the basement stairs and call David, her daddy. His voice still sounds congested, but also languid, like he has just had sex. I tell him that Cloris is having, in her words, her worst day ever, and that we are going to whisk her back home.

"Oh, she says that all the time. Once she told me that my goodnight kiss felt like maggots crawling on her. I just have to keep telling myself that she was born to be a goth. Tell her how much you can't stand Hannah Montana and you'll have her in the palm of your hand. Please keep her 'til, like, dinnertime at least?"

He's off the phone before I can ask him who Hannah Montana is. Still, I return to the laundry room and announce, apropos of nothing, that I cannot stand Hannah Montana.

"Ha ha ha!" Cloris goes, a little girl at last. "I want her to explode! Sage says she wishes Hannah Montana was her mom. But Sage is dumb."

"Who's Hannah Montana?" Glen asks, panicked. "Who's Sage?"

"They're people from television," I say.

"Sage is *not* from television," Cloris says. "She's from the condo beside ours. Her mom is, like, seventy.

They had to cook up Sage in a science lab and then they fed her to her old lady mom and that is how she was born."

Glen is shaking his head. Confused. Pissed off that there is always, always more to know. Nothing can be done.

"You know what," I say finally. "Let's bring the TV upstairs. Let's put it in our bedroom. We need a TV."

Glen moves to help me but I wave him away, already bending at the knees, slowly lifting this old, dusty, cracked, black plastic idiot box.

Tycoon

As a child, Lyle was loud, sweaty, nervous, scary-skinny, prone to migraines and insomnia. When he finally did nod off at night, his parents would pad away and sit silently in the kitchen, his mother weepy and his father stunned to stone, the two of them exhausted hostages.

Lyle finished high school with a 97% average; he got scholarships to every major university in the country. He chose the University of Toronto. He picked a whole bunch of unrelated courses.

The summer before school started, a choreographer saw Lyle dancing alone at Club Colby's. He approached Lyle, rhapsodized about Lyle's innate grace and physical lyricism, and asked Lyle there and then to join his dance troupe. Lyle loved dance, constant motion of any kind, and so he joined the troupe. He dropped out of school.

Rehearsals were endless. There were six dancers in the troupe, three women, three men. There was much flinging, soaring, tumbling and gasping. The studio was hot and airless; the windows wept with condensation. All the dancers nursed multiple injuries. The troupe was fraught with frantic love affairs and lots of squabbles.

Every few hours, Lyle and the choreographer would adjourn to a stairwell where the choreographer would lap Lyle's sweat. While he was lapped at, Lyle would catch his breath and stave off fainting.

One of the male dancers came down with PCP pneumonia, an AIDS-defining illness. The choreographer found a replacement, a red-headed boy with a lithe torso and massive buttocks. The choreographer was taken with the red-headed boy in the way he had been with Lyle.

The choreographer introduced a new sequence: Lyle would do a blind back flip off a platform to begin it.

The first time Lyle attempted the blind back flip, he landed on his head and broke his neck. He was in a coma for seven weeks; when he awoke, he told his parents of a long dream he'd had in which he was locked in a closet stuffed with crinoline.

Once Lyle was stable, his parents brought him back to Winnipeg. He learned to walk again. Within a year, he could work the riding lawn mower and waltz with his mother through the living room. The choreographer called once, for a minute, from a Berlin airport. Lyle wished him the best in his choreographic pursuits and, when he hung up, struggled to put a face to the choreographer's name.

Lyle was no longer noisy and nervous. Doctors assured him that he was, apart from a numb left thumb and forefinger, neurologically intact, but he was a markedly different person. He was placid now, deliberate, wistful. He napped. His parents fell in love with him; they went fishing together, sightseeing throughout the Canadian Shield, strawberry-picking in Hadashville. In the evenings the three of them would drink rum-and-cokes and sing along to Marty Robbins records.

Lyle still had desire, but it was diffuse now. He could love a man or woman readily, sparely; he could also be sidetracked for months by the work of an interesting, unfamiliar writer or a particular approach to calisthenics. This didn't sit well with most of his partners, who misread his equanimity as deceit. Lyle briefly had a girlfriend who refused to believe that he was truly bisexual and not just a gutless gay man. Lyle had tried to convince her otherwise – wasn't their sex always inventive and fun? The girlfriend conceded that the sex was good. So good, in fact, that it seemed to her that Lyle was overcompensating. Whenever she looked deeply into his eyes, she said, all she saw were penises.

Fifteen years passed. Lyle worked a few inconsequential jobs: convenience store cashier, condo concierge. Always, after a few weeks, his mother would start to lament Lyle's absence at home, so Lyle would quit the job to spend time with her.

Last summer, Lyle's mother died, suddenly but softly, while reading on the veranda. His father, a dainty, sentimental man who loved his wife lavishly, took to his bed, rising only in the evenings to eat toast, drink vodka, and sometimes tearfully sing old Irish folk songs to himself.

Lyle grew listless too. Since the accident, there had been a sad aspect to Lyle, but it was held in check by the lovely levity of his family. Now, with his mother gone and his father dead to the world, Lyle could only sit on the bare veranda and wonder if the most, the only, interesting part of himself had long ago gone the way of the feeling in his thumb and forefinger.

He decided one night as he watched his small father sleep to dive headlong into a new career, any career. He'd find a new, fizzy milieu, filled with gossip and humour, and every night he'd bring stories of the day's shenanigans home with him, filling his faltering father's life too.

+

Lyle was in Shoppers Drug Mart buying a big bag of butterscotch candies for his father, when he saw the sign saying that the cosmetics section was looking for a new counter person. He went up to a woman in a black pantsuit who was arranging a display of women's hair colouring kits that had tipped over.

He asked the woman – "Nathalie" read her name-tag – if cosmetics was still looking for help. She looked him up and down as though he were wearing a long coat of purple fur.

"Well, yes, we sure are!" Nathalie said. "Do you think you might want to become a part of our team?"

Lyle turned the idea over in his head a good thirty seconds or so. "Yes," he said finally. "I think I might. Like it. To be part of your team."

Nathalie clapped her hands together and bolted over to the intercom. "NANDITA! NOW!" she screamed into the microphone, shaking the building.

+

Lyle and Nathalie sat on folding chairs in a tiny stock-room. Nathalie was fanning herself with a short stack of resumés from other applicants.

"What do you think you can bring to our team?" she asked.

Lyle considered the question while also giving Nathalie a good once-over. She was a small-boned thing, but she'd let herself go. She was a little "sloppy," as his mother would have said reluctantly in a whisper; Nathalie's stomach strained against the brass buttons of her blazer. Otherwise, she was immaculately groomed. Short, spiky, bleach-blonde hair, excessive makeup for midday but all of it artfully applied, perfectly white, square teeth that may or may not have been dentures.

"More than anything," he said quietly, "I would like to help women feel good about themselves. It would be nice to be a man in a staff of women, helping lady people – ladies, I should say. Sorry, I have a brain issue, sort of."

"Oh no!" Nathalie gasped. "That's awful. Is it life-threatening?"

"No, no. I had an accident, a long time ago. Anyway, yes, I would like to help ladies to really...flourish."

Nathalie sighed with approval. She did a little upper body shimmy in her seat.

Lyle believed he understood Nathalie completely already. He'd dated several women like her: manic and beaming. There was probably a stolen library book somewhere in Nathalie's apartment, a book on how to be an effective people person. Which was all well and good, but when these specific women crash? Broken china. Binge eating. Waterhouse reproductions torn to bits on linty bedroom floors. The woman who saw penises in Lyle's eyes was one of these women.

"I really like to think that I understand women, some women anyway. My best friend was my mum."

"Stop! My peepers are welling up!"

She wiped away an onyx tear. "So much for water-proof mascara! Thanks for nothing, Max Factor! Why can't you be more like Lyle here?"

Lyle smiled. Nathalie's tears had made Lyle tearful. It didn't take much since the accident; "emotional liability" is what the doctors called this easy tearfulness.

"Know what? Fuck it! I like you. Let's go meet the team!"

They went back to the floor. At the counter were two tall, beautiful women, both in black pantsuits.

"This is Nandita," Nathalie said, gesturing at the younger of the two, a Southeast Asian woman with perfect skin. "Nandita is just great. Her mother and father are like royalty in India."

"Nathalie! We're *Persian*," purred Nandita with a toss of her lustrous hair.

Lyle shook Nandita's tiny, icy hand.

"And this here is...I'm trying to think of a fitting word for you, Marnie."

"Oh, c'mon," said Marnie. "I know you have a word for me."

"Actually, know what? I have two: veteran vixen. This is our veteran vixen, Marnie. She has been here much longer than any of us."

"Thanks for emphasizing that, Nathalie. It's a tremendous source of pride, my professional dead end."

Marnie crackled with wit and intellect, Lyle thought. She would be fun to play pool with. He liked the idea of Marnie warming to him, eventually inviting him over for poker, daring to share with him her big scrapbook filled with pictures torn from magazines, of gorgeous horses ridden by jubilant cowgirls.

"There are also a few evening and weekend girls," Nathalie said. "But you'll seldom work with them. Unless Marnie or Nandita is sick."

"I'm sick a lot," Nandita said. "I have no immune system. They thought maybe I had AIDS when I was little."

"Please don't say 'AIDS' on the floor, Nandita," Nathalie said, still smiling.

Lyle would start the next day. Until he could be fitted for his own black pantsuit, he was to wear his own dark suit ("Please, no appliqués! One of the weekend girls came in with ice cream cone appliqués on her blazer and I made her tear them off in front of me!").

When Lyle got home, his father was up, drinking. Lyle told his father all about his new job, the lovely women he'd be working with.

"Makeup," his father said absently. "Your mum didn't care for makeup. When she wore makeup, she said she felt like a...oh, what is it called when a man gets all dressed up like a lady?"

"I forget," Lyle said. "I know what you mean, though."

+

Nathalie was training Lyle, badly. She kept prefacing her tutorials with "of course, you probably already know this," then glazing over the crucial details, giggling into her hands. She kept doing this, even after Lyle explained to her that he knew almost nothing pertinent to the job. It had been years since he'd even used a cash register.

After lunch, she left him on his own with Marnie and Nandita.

"What's your background?" Nandita asked Lyle.

"Do you mean professionally?"

"No. Like, are you a Jew?"

"A Jew? No. God, no – I pronounced "synagogue" with *j*s instead of hard *g*'s until a few months ago. No, I'm a pretty boring mishmash: Irish and English. I'd quite like to be Jewish. Such a vibrant, ancient culture."

"And you're homo, right?"

"Geez, Nan, lay off," Marnie said, reading a flyer. "Why don't you take a rectal swab while you're at it."

"It's okay, Marnie. Actually, I'm bisexual."

Marnie cocked an eyebrow.

"Get out!" said Nandita. "So are you, like, *Oh my God, I'm so bi, I'll have to flip a coin?*"

"No. I just take things person by person these days. When I was younger, I was pretty much gay, though."

"And then what happened?" Nandita asked, baffled.

"I fell on my head."

"Nice one," Marnie said, laughing and patting Lyle on the back. "That's exactly how I explain away my first marriage, too."

Nandita still looked confused. She would definitely marry young, Lyle thought. Marry young and then face a moderate mortal test of some sort – a baby with a withered arm, severe basement flooding – after which she'd perceive herself anew, as a learned survivor, even as her deportment indicated that she was exactly as insulated and self-absorbed as she'd ever been. Just a hunch he had.

Nandita retrieved a slim cigarette from her purse and took Marnie by the arm. "We're going to duck out for a quick ciggie, Lyle."

"We can't leave him alone on his first day, Nan," Marnie said.

"Go, go. I'll be fine. Really."

Marnie grabbed a pack of Player's Lights from under the cash register.

A woman approached the cash with a box of hair dye from the promotional display. Lyle didn't know how to ring it in, so he put the box in a bag and just gave it to her.

+

"I didn't know how to ring it in so I just gave it to her," Lyle told his father, who was sitting up in bed, drinking.

"You did her a good turn," his father said. "Why can't people do good turns for each other more often? 'Member how the three of us used to shovel all the driveways on our street in the winter? Very few good people kicking around anymore."

+

Lyle accidentally rang through some nail polish for $8,990 on a credit card.

"Just do a pur corr," Marnie said.

"A what?"

"A purchase correction."

Lyle looked at Marnie and shrugged. Marnie mimed wringing his neck.

"Oh my Jesus God," she said. "I'll do it. Watch me."

After the customer left, Marnie folded her arms and leaned against the counter. "Nathalie said you were some kind of industry veteran, but you don't even know what a pur corr is?"

"No. I'm not an industry veteran."

Marnie snorted.

"You totally conned her, didn't you? Smooooth! Have you even worked retail before?"

"Well, not *retail* retail, really."

"Ha! I totally called it the very first day," she said. "I knew it. Another case of the smiley wacko going with her gut. God. Like I've said before – she certainly has a lot of gut to go with, but her instincts are the shits."

"Please don't get me fired. This job is actually kind of important to me."

"Ooh, reach for the stars, honey. Slackers unite! Don't you worry. I've got your back."

Lyle liked Marnie. Her dark, close-set eyes made her look perpetually caught in deep thought. She was exactly Lyle's age: 35. He wondered what it was she would rather be doing with her life. He didn't want to scare her away by admitting that he could not think of anything he'd rather be doing with *his* life.

"Let's go have a cigarette," Marnie said.

"I don't smoke."

"Something else I'll have to teach you to do. C'mon."

+

"I smoked my first cigarette," Lyle said into the darkness of his father's bedroom.

"You woke me up to tell me that? Oh, chum. Oh, my boy. Go smoke a pack and get back to me."

+

117

One day Nandita tumbled down an escalator clad in stiletto heels and broke an arm. She met a man while convalescing. They quickly got engaged, and Nandita was never heard from again. Nathalie insisted on meeting with Marnie and Lyle so that the three of them could talk about their feelings and process Nandita's absence.

"I feel like I've lost a child," Nathalie said. "Don't you feel like you've lost a child, Marnie?"

"No. I would've been twelve at the time of her birth."

"What about you, Lyle?"

"I barely knew Nandita."

"Well, I'm sad," Nathalie continued, undeterred. "I've had a lot of hardship in life. I may or may not have told you that I was born with my intestines on the outside of my body. You'd think that would have toughened me up. But I'm still all mush."

Nathalie suggested holding off on hiring a new person. They all needed time to grieve Nandita, and it would be impossible for a newbie to break through the yoke of their shared grief.

Marnie was amenable; she didn't like new people as a rule. Lyle was flattered that Marnie would be willing to co-pilot with him.

Lyle and Marnie quickly developed an affectionately snarky rapport. By the middle of that workweek, he'd grown insular with Marnie; he stopped relaying the day's events to his sleeping father.

Marnie was a fixture at a local sports bar. On Friday, Marnie asked Lyle if he'd like to tag along. Lyle hadn't been out socially with anyone other than his parents for more than a year. He jumped at the chance.

At the bar, Marnie poured from a big pitcher of draught and made a toast.

"To the grieving process," Marnie said, rolling her eyes protractedly as she took her first sip. "Doesn't Nathalie make you just want to saw your head off?"

"She's certainly energetic. I can see how she might start to grate over time. I don't hate her though. Is part of your distaste because you'd rather be manager yourself?"

"Are you kidding me? I've been trying to extricate myself from that place for years. Last thing I want to do is get in even deeper."

"What would you rather be doing?"

"Oh, God. I don't know. Nothing specific. Mainly, I just want to get away from fluorescent lighting."

Lyle liked that answer. Marnie rolled her head around; her neck made cracking sounds. She went outside for a smoke. Lyle stayed behind. He'd only just started smoking, and could go for hours without one.

Marnie returned, bursting with renewed anti-Nathalie sentiment.

"She really is one of the stupidest people I've ever met," Marnie said before she'd even sat. "And one of the most condescending. Stupid and condescending is an unbearable combo."

"She isn't the most perceptive person, no. But I haven't experienced her as condescending."

"That's because you're a man. Oh yeah, it's really as basic as that. It's only a matter of time before she asks you out."

Lyle scoffed and threw himself back in his chair, inadvertently knocking the head of the woman behind him. She shrieked. He apologized profusely.

"That's how Nathalie got the job, you know," Marnie continued. "She was at another Shoppers way out in Northern Ontario, and she fucked a district manager or someone important. When he wouldn't leave his wife for her, she threatened to tell his wife that he'd repeatedly slipped Nathalie GHB and had sex with her lifeless body. So they gave her a promotion and got her the hell out of town."

"Wow. How do you know all this?"

"I've been at Shoppers eleven years. I'm very *plugged in.*"

Even though Marnie was empirically attractive, Lyle wasn't drawn to her sexually, and Marnie seemed to have zero interest in romance of any kind. She seemed the kind of person who would find ultimate sensual fulfillment in sitting in a hot tub carved into the side of a cold mountain, dreamily allowing the bubbly heat and brisk wind to confuse her flesh. Lyle was happy to have a new friend.

They got drunk. Their banter got sillier and sillier. They played Would You Rather? until last call.

Would you rather lose a finger or go down on Carol Channing? Would you rather kill your parents and siblings or pimp out your children? Would you rather go to some obvious tropical hotspot with Nathalie or spend two weeks in a minimum security prison?

+

Tacked to the bulletin board in the stockroom was an open invite to Nathalie's housewarming party, end of the month.

Pleeease come! Bring as many people as you want! Lots of yummy homemade snacks! A half-page of other exclamatory statements followed.

Marnie mercilessly mocked Nathalie's hysterical neediness for several hours, until Lyle couldn't help but join in. The mind did reel at what Nathalie's interpretation of *yummy homemade snacks* might be, Lyle conceded.

"Exactly," said Marnie. "You just know there's going to be at least one pube in every dish."

+

Nathalie stopped Lyle in the hallway.

"How are things? How's 'twosies' working out?"

"Good! Great!"

"Oh, yay! Are you coming to my housewarming?"

"Umm. Very probably."

"Very probably? With so much advance notice? It's essential that you come. Really."

"Okay."

"Great. You're blowing my mind! Yay!"

Back at the counter, Lyle asked Marnie if there was absolutely any way she might consider going to Nathalie's party with him.

"Ha!" she said. "Are we playing Would You Rather? again? Whatever it is, I pick the other option."

"Really? Even if we went ironically?"

"Sorry, buddy. You can totally come over afterward and tell me all about it, though."

+

Lyle's father was in a bathrobe, propped up against the side of the beige recliner, drinking.

"I get to go to a work party, Dad."

"That's nice. Do you ever wonder how it could come to be that your life is all about one person, one thing, and then, when it's gone, you're just a carcass?"

"We all feel that way sometimes. You're not a carcass, Dad."

"Maybe. Maybe not."

+

Lyle slicked back his hair and threw on a baby-blue cable knit sweater.

Nathalie's little house was deep in the east end. Lyle got there just after nine o'clock. The front door was unlocked. He knocked and walked in. Silence.

Nathalie, clad in a urine-coloured rayon dress, was sitting on the living room couch. Empty beer bottles all along the edge of the boomerang-shaped coffee table.

"I asked sixty-three people to my housewarming party," she said. "Thirty-six confirmed, verbally or via email. And nobody came. Except for you. I knew you'd come. You're an evolved person. I know that. That is something that this lady here knows."

Lyle looked around. All of the furniture seemed undersized and precarious. He set his gift bag, three big scented candles, on the floor and sat on a wobbly rocking chair.

"I'm really sorry that your party didn't turn out as planned."

"I don't understand. Why do I gross people out? I try and try."

"People are just really, really busy. And there's that big baseball card convention happening at the rec centre this weekend, remember?"

She smiled. She wept.

"If I didn't have my faith in God, I'd have been carried out to sea like a...Like a...Who even knows. Did you know that I'm a Christian?"

"No."

"Of course, how could you know? I keep my faith out of the workplace. But Jesus Christ is my husband. That makes me sound like a nun. I'm not a nun. Jesus Christ is my boyfriend. Eww, that sounds tacky. He's my roommate. I love Him." She daubed at her eyes with the hem of her dress, exposing flesh-tone panties.

"I'd offer you some yummy snacks but I threw them all out when I realized that the COCKSUCK-ERS WEREN'T GONNA SHOW UP! I'm sorry. Praise Him. I receive Him."

Lyle leaned forward.

"Can I heat you up some soup? Or get you settled into bed or something?"

"You're so nice. I knew from the start that you were bound for glory. We're lucky to have you at Shoppers. Do you want a blow job?"

"Umm..."

"I absolutely did not just say that. I'm sorry. Nathalie is sorry. Last Shoppers I was at, all the girls hated me because men always find me intensely desirable. At the Christmas party, somebody shit in my purse. True story. That really, really hurt me."

She stood. Lyle worried that she was about to stab him.

"I'm going to show you something," she said. "I've never shown anyone what I'm going to show you."

She led the way, down the hall, last room on the right. She knelt on the floor and pulled a sandwich baggie out from under the bed. From the baggie, she took out several little bones. Chicken bones, looked like. And then a little bell. And a rolled-up scrap of paper.

"It says in the Bible," Nathalie said, solemnly spreading out the bones, "that it's okay to practise black magic as long as you're a Christian and as long as you also practise white magic. Or as long as you're a white person. I forget. Something like that."

"Where does it say that in the Bible?"

"Well, I can't give you chapter and verse. I'm not a fanatic. Anyway, I wanted to show you this. It'll give you a leg up on the competition when you become a – cosmetics tycoon."

"I don't want to be a cosmetics tycoon."

"Whatever. It'll help you gain revenge on your enemies."

"I don't have any enemies."

"As if! God, work with me a little. There must be *somebody*."

Lyle thought of the choreographer, and the blind back flip that was almost certainly intended to cause him injury and end his life as a dancer. Or, at the very least, to end his life as the choreographer's boyfriend.

"Go ahead," he said.

Nathalie drew a dramatic breath.

"Now, I performed a spell similar to this one on all the horrible girls at the Sudbury Shoppers. Two days later, they shared a pizza and all of them came down with E. coli. And one went septic and almost died. And when Nandita came up to me awhile ago and said that my breasts were asymmetrical but that it kind of worked, like when you wear a little earring on one ear and a big earring on the other, naturally I had to take action. Next day she tumbled down the escalator."

Lyle didn't know whether to laugh, bolt, indulge, or call the police. He'd dated a couple of white witches, and a nudist who wouldn't leave the house without consulting the I Ching, but nothing like this.

"This spell is for a certain someone we both know who has only ever been rude and demeaning to me," Nathalie said with strange serenity, as if she were on-air with a DJ, dedicating a Celine Dion song to a new lover.

Nathalie stood. "With these bones I now do crush," she said slowly. Then she stomped on the chicken bones, again and again, in her bare feet. The bones became blood-flecked. Finally, she stopped.

"I call upon the Ancient Ones from the poison abyss to do my bidding. I invoke Cthulhu, God of Anger, and the creatures of the underworld, gnarled and with knives for teeth. Hear me! Hear me now! Defile her flesh. Cause her to rot."

"That's really not very nice at all. Marnie's a great person once you get to know—"

"Shut the fuck up! I'm not finished!"

She shut her eyes. She rang the little bell three times.

"There we go!" said Nathalie, as if she had just finished frosting a cake. "We are good to go!"

"Oh. Man. What did you wish upon...the victim?"

"A little of this, a little of that. Let's go to Burger King!"

+

Lyle grew nauseous when Marnie didn't show for work on Monday. He called her house again and again. No answer. He was certain that she was lying dead on the kitchen floor, already stiff. He was an accomplice to magic murder.

He'd been home an hour, sitting in the dark on the edge of his father's bed, when Marnie called.

"You called me like eighty times today," she said. "What the fuck?"

"Marnie. Sweetheart. Thank God. I was so worried."

"Chill. I'm fine. My mother died yesterday."

"No! Oh!"

"It's okay. She was a bitch. But she left me everything. Like 300K, when all is said and done. Soooo, guess who's going back to school to learn animal husbandry? Guess who's through with Shoppers fucking Drug Mart?"

Marnie was braying with glee. Lyle was confused. Marnie had, indeed, experienced tragedy. But that tragedy had, in turn, changed Marnie's life for the better. Maybe's Nathalie's spell was more complicated than she'd let on; maybe she was too proud to admit that there was a benevolent back end to the spell. Or maybe Nathalie was just a shitty sorceress.

"I'm so happy for you, Marnie. You're sure you feel okay?"

"I feel fantastic."

"And your – flesh. Is your flesh intact?"

"What? Is my flesh intact? What the fuck are you talking about? Anyway, make yourself pretty, 'cuz we're going to karaoke tonight to celebrate!"

Lyle felt dazed. He told her he'd get back to her about karaoke and hung up.

He paced the living room. He thought of his small, leisurely life. He went to the coat rack and retrieved the package Nathalie had given him on Saturday night.

Lyle went into his father's room. He sat beside his father's sleeping form. He shook his father awake. His father didn't startle; he never startled. He simply opened his eyes.

"Yes. What?" his father said.

"Dad, what if...do you think...do you think that if you practise black magic for, y'know, wholesome reasons, it's okay if you practise black magic?"

"Christ. Are you reading off of one of those Alzheimer's questionnaires you get at the pharmacy? Yes, I know what day it is. No, I don't believe in magic. I don't have Alzheimer's, Lyle."

"I know that."

Lyle emptied the contents of the baggie – the bones and the bell – onto the bed.

"Dad, I need you to try something for me. I need you to...envision me—"

"Oh, Jesus, Lyle, I'm too old to envision things."

"Please, just try. I need you to envision me at my all-time happiest and most...happy."

Lyle's father sighed a long sigh.

"Yeah, okay. And?"

"And then I need you to say, 'I crush bones over you,'" he said. "No, wait. That's wrong. You need to say, 'I crush thee like a bone.' Shit. What was it? Oh! 'With these bones I now do crush.' And you have to say that with real fervor, real zeal, you know what I mean? And then I need you to—"

"Good Christ, Lyle. I'm not going to say all that. That's more than I usually say in a whole year. And what are these little crumbs and sticks you've gotten all over the bed? Isn't this a nice mess."

Lyle looked down at the bones and bell. He wiped them into his palm.

"I'm sorry, Dad. It was just this reverse curse the girls at work were doing. A happiness curse."

"Yeah, well. Happiness *is* a curse, they got that right. Because when happiness ends...Christ, my ass is all pins 'n' needles. Anyway, I'm not going to envision you one way or another. You're good the way you are. Go smoke a cigarette. Or call up one of those makeup girls you run around with. You leave your dad alone now."

Lyle could think of nothing better to do, so he took his father's advice. He took the cordless, went outside, and lit up a smoke. He called Marnie back. She answered on the first ring.

THE TINKER

Joan fell down in the sunroom. She was standing on the footstool, trying to water her one and only house-plant. She lost her balance, her cheek smashed against the bookcase, and now she had a bad gash on her face. Joan. Single, bald, and wounded.

I was in the kitchen when it happened. She came to me, bleeding. This sort of thing happens constantly. The two rooms I rent from her are spacious and well-lit. Cheap as hell, cable, phone and laundry included. But if I'd known that I'd have to tend to Joan all the time – well. I don't know.

I bandaged her.

"Oh, that was so jarring," she said. "For some reason, it evokes memories of the sexual abuse I suffered as a pre-teen. I'm so shaken," she said. "Please hold me."

I held her, trying not to sigh from the tedium of this particular gambit of Joan's. She wept silently. I thought that might, for once, be the end of her daily breakdown, but as I gently let loose my arms, she started in with her pre-teen sex abuse lament.

Joan's mother walked in on her once when Joan was doing up her training bra, and Joan screamed. That was her sex abuse. When she recounted it yet again awhile ago, I said that most people wouldn't consider that sexual abuse.

"It was all in the execution!" she screamed at the time. "My mother bought me that training bra, and when she saw me wearing the training bra, sure she apologized and shut the door, but you could tell that my embarrassment thrilled her, sexually! And the very next day, she bought me a pom-pom skirt!"

I managed to mollify Joan and I returned to my room.

+

I'm sitting at my drawing board, staring at my current work-in-progress. I am an artist, I think. Yes, I am almost certain that I am an artist.

I use the Spirograph, and then I integrate other ominous, evocative images. The cumulative effect is, against all odds, often quite thrilling. I just finished my second piece. It took a year and a half. Several red Spirograph circles, a screaming cow, and a tampon. It's called *I Have Seen the Wind*.

Progress is slow on the new piece. So far, it's just one blue Spirograph circle. No title yet. I will persist, but if this is to be my process, this endless dither-ing…I will try my best not to question my process.

Joan doesn't mind that I'm on welfare. Actually, she thinks it indicates strength of character. Joan has been on all kinds of social assistance. She's rattled off all of her afflictions. But the only ones I remember are alopecia, and that she supposedly gets a concussion if she ever has to use an elevator.

Part of me would like to get a little office job or something. But I can't until I've fully transitioned; my transition feels too precious and porcelain to enact in some mundane workplace. I've gone from Tracy to Trace, on my way to Trey. But I don't know if I want to be entirely Trey. Mainly, I would like to be very austere and post-modern, genderless. I've always loved Laurie Anderson. But I don't know.

For now, I have my circles and suits and two well-lit rooms. I'm somewhat content, I think.

+

Joan has a new friend, Myra. Joan passed out while waiting in the checkout line at Pharma Plus. Myra caught her artfully, caught her with one arm.

Myra says she is a medium and a Celtic tinker. When we met, she took my hand in both of hers and pressed it to her heart. Her chest was sweaty.

Myra stayed for supper tonight. Joan asked me to join them. But I already had my hotplate going. I heard Joan using the blender a lot.

I listened in on their after-dinner conversation. Myra would say something like, "Joan, your pain is pre-ordained," and Joan would say, "Oh my God, that is so true!" And then Myra asked if Joan ever knew a man named John.

"Oh, my God!" Joan said. "Yes! My father's barber was named John. And John the barber used to give me marshmallows while I waited for my father to get his hair cut. I'm certain it was a kind of seduction. Recounting it makes me want to bathe. And then I knew a John in university, and he had testicular cancer but he survived. Many Johns, yes. Many, many Johns."

"As it is written," Myra said.

"Yes, as it is written," Joan replied. "Written where?"

"That's enough for tonight. I love you, Joan."

I'm glad that Joan has someone to else to talk to, but this Myra is really the limit. I hope Joan isn't giving her money. Joan used to have a cleaning lady who would brazenly steal from Joan – cash, a whole drawer full of panties – and whenever Joan confronted her, the cleaning lady would tell Joan that Joan was imagining things because Joan was insane. And Joan wants so badly to be insane. So she kept the cleaning lady. Eventually, the cleaning lady drank herself to death.

I have to pee. I abandon my work-in-progress and head to the bathroom.

The door opens while I'm sitting on the toilet. I yell a prohibitive "hello."

"I'm so sorry! Tracy – is it Tracy?'"

"Trace."

"Trace. Right. Trace."

Myra's still standing there, staring.

"How are you?"

"I'm fine. I'm peeing."

"Oh yeah. That's great. So. Joan tells me you're a female-to-male."

"Sort of. I'm. Umm. Intergendered. I'm into gender fluidity. And gender, like, denialism. And...Laurie Anderson."

She nods. Clacks a fingernail against the faucet. "Oh yeah. That's great. Y'know, since I'm already butting in as you pee, can I just tell you a little something?"

I tear off a wad of toilet paper.

"Sure. Just give me a minute."

"It can't wait. I'll forget. When prophecy hits me, I have to deliver the message immediately or I forget."

"Okay. What?"

"Spirit is telling me all about you, Trace. Spirit is saying that if you become a man, you will know fulfillment in every way and will also make inroads playing the stock market. Spirit is also saying – oh! Ha ha!"

"What? What is it?"

"Sorry. A little joke between me and Spirit. Anyway, Spirit is saying that if you decide to remain a she/he—"

"An intergendered person," I amend.

"Yes, right, of course, sorry. An intergendered person. If you choose to remain an intergendered person, something terrible will happen."

I wipe and flush. "I see. Tell me."

"Spirit says that if you stay an intergendered person, you will be decapitated when you are thirty-six. I'm so sorry."

I laugh, a huge, honking laugh unfamiliar to me. Joan yells from downstairs. Asks if everything is okay.

"We're good," Myra says. "I'm just helping Trace in the bathroom."

"Oh. I also need some help in the bathroom," Joan says. "Can someone carry me to the toilet? I feel unsteady."

"One sec," Myra says.

I wash my hands with Joan's tiny clam-shaped soap. Myra watches me dreamily, as though I were a fish wafting through an aquarium. I make a big show of lathering my hands and rinsing them thoroughly; for some reason, it is important to me that Myra sees me as fastidious. Perhaps, I reason, if Myra sees me as fastidious, a disciplined hand-washer, she may revise her decapitation prophecy. "Is there, like, a third option?" I ask Myra as she hands me one of Joan's tiny pink hand towels.

"A third option?" Myra asks, astonished, maybe even offended.

"Yeah, like, what if I do, like, a seasonal gender thing? Six months as a man, six months as a woman? Or Spring/Summer, man, Fall/Winter, woman? I'm just kind of riffing here, but you get the idea?"

Myra sighs. Shuts her eyes.

"Spirit hates ambivalence. Spirit says that if you don't become a man or a woman, full stop, calamity will ensue. Ambivalence breeds ambivalence, which then breeds insanity. You'll be in the grocery store. You wouldn't be able to decide which kind of margarine to buy. You'll mull and mull. Then you'll start screaming, and they'll nab you, and you will be institutionalized forever. This is what Spirit is saying. Please, Trace, dear heart, please pick one and go with it."

"Thank you. I'll certainly give it my best shot."

Myra reaches deep into a pocket on her tie-dyed skirt, fishes out her card: name and number in pink calligraphy, bracketed by pink seahorses. She smiles and winks as she hands it to me. I stand there, emotionless. She finally goes away.

Myra bugs me, I decide. I'm only twenty; it is thoughtless and psychically unethical of her to spook me into conventional gender identity while I'm barely out of my teens and haven't yet decided on the simplest things. I don't yet know if I like earth tones. I don't yet know if I like air conditioning!

I hear her grunt as she hoists Joan into her arms.

"Oh, thank you, Myra. I'm in so much physical and emotional pain. Does Spirit maybe say that aromatherapy might be helpful for me?"

"Spirit sleeps," Myra says, breathy from exertion.

"Oh. Okay. I can wait 'til Spirit wakes up."

Back in my room, seated at my drawing board, I add another circle to my work-in-progress. Two blue circles now. My cheeks burn from this brazenness. Another circle, a red one. I can absolutely be intergendered without having my head come off at thirty-six!

Then – why not? Really, why not? Why the hell not? I sketch a little tub of margarine. Becel. Becel is, without a doubt, my preferred brand of margarine, thank you very much, Myra.

I stand back from the board. Could this piece be finished so fast? I think it might very well be.

THE TINKER
IN LOVE

Like her late mother, Myra worked as a psychic. Charming and persuasive, she did good business. People left her living room tearful and satisfied, despite the absence of any hard information during the session with her. She'd appeared on several local television chat shows. She touted herself variously as a Celtic tinker, a medium, and a spirit healer with hinted-at-but-never-specified First Nations heritage.

Myra was a fraud, but otherwise quite ethically high-minded. As such, her fraudulence was starting to wear on her.

Her mother, Thelma, was a real psychic who helped cops and clients find buried babies, lost jewelry, and deadbeat dads. The old women in her neighbourhood would run when they saw her, so afraid were they that she'd forecast their time and place of death right there on the sidewalk. Thelma seldom spoke her visions, so when she did, you knew she meant business. She only got it sort of wrong once: she told the police they would find a blonde woman's severed head in someone's backyard, and when the cops got to the scene, they found that the head in question belonged to a Barbie doll. The incident didn't really count, however, because Thelma was already bedridden by then and often got mixed up as to what day it was.

Thelma was fifty when Myra was born; frail to begin with, Thelma was simply too worn out to run after a child. It was all she could do to chainsmoke and listen to the radio, and when little Myra came around, wanting attention or a snack, Thelma would shoo her away and tell her to go to bed, regardless of the hour.

When Thelma learned that she was terminal with lung cancer, she wrote out a long-range forecast for her only child. It was the least she could do. She was careful not to pull any punches, however; she would give her girl an overview replete with all possible joy and calamity so Myra would know when to aggressively exercise free will and when to simply sit back and enjoy.

Myra was only ten at the time, but already Thelma perceived an indolence in Myra, a tendency to loll that could only lead to dissatisfaction later on down the line. Maybe this list of predictions would be the kick in the pants that Myra needed.

+

You will struggle in school unless you really apply yourself. You're a natural chatterbox, which can sometimes be a good thing, but your teachers will watch you prattling on about this, that and the other thing, and wonder if maybe you are borderline retarded. Please, Myra. Button your lips and focus on the task at hand.

With no second sight of her own, Myra had no way of verifying her mother's hunches. And she was so angry at her mother for dying and leaving Myra with her dotty, maudlin father that she flouted most of Thelma's early instructions. Myra was tested upwards of a dozen times for learning disability. "If A = N, then whatever. Fuck off!"

You aren't especially pretty – at least, not at first glance. And this next bit will seem trivial, but: without constant, careful attention to your appearance, you will always look slightly greasy. Your father has terribly oily skin, which only grows oilier under stress. At the altar on our wedding day, I felt as though I were marrying an olive.

Nonetheless, boys will sniff you out. They'll find your lazy way alluring, relaxing, they'll want to go bowling with you, and then do various other things to your various orifices. One of them will be named Niall, with a long foreskin that makes his penis look like an anteater. Among his early sexual requests will be that you bounce naked upon his father's old pogo stick, making your pendulous breasts thwap about wildly.

Of course, I advise you to steer clear, read books, do sit-ups, garden. But you like a lot of attention, so you'll let the boys hang around. Niall will get you pregnant. When you tell him, he will pound the dashboard of his car with his fist and curse. Then he'll offer to marry you. Two days later, you'll fall on black ice and miscarry. Marriage called off, Niall will become a pharmacist, and you'll reel for a good while, stunned by the sudden turn of events, and by the fact that events can turn so suddenly. Thereafter, you and Niall will pretend not to know each other, absurd as that seems, when you pick up prescriptions at Niall's Shoppers.

These young years, Myra, are perhaps the most pivotal of your life. So much will be decided. If you bear down and work hard, you can carve out a lovely little life for yourself. You are NOT the kind of person who can coast. You're not an innately lucky person. If you do nothing, nothing will happen for you. You might as well be a goat or a salad – that is how inconsequential your life will be if you do nothing.

Myra ran on impulse in her teens and twenties. When she was twenty-two, her father died in his sleep. She didn't notice for two days.

There was this woman who ran the telemarketing company where Myra worked for a few months, this small woman with huge, glassy green eyes who made Myra's stomach arc and plummet with excitement whenever she leaned over Myra's workstation. These feelings were new to Myra, and she quickly came to count upon them for sustenance. Then the woman found another job. Myra slowly forgot about her.

Sometimes Myra did feel a higher calling, a spirit beseeching her to meditate and pore over sacred texts. Other times, she wanted only to drink cheap domestic beer, and see what kind of predictable trouble she and her chirpy, yearning, acne-scarred girlfriends could get into down at Ruby Tuesday's.

She was confounded by her mother's advice. Yes, the exchange with Niall Hyslop happened exactly as outlined; she did slip in a parking lot in high heels and miscarry. The whole bit about crying in the gutter, though...sure, she kind of coasted for awhile, working at Safeway, taping *Days of Our Lives* every day to watch when she got home each evening, and eating Kraft Dinner on a TV table positioned at the edge of her bed. But she was never homeless, never ill, and never in trouble with the law, except for that one time when she got lost on Gerrard Street, and stood still for a moment to get her bearings, and a cop pulled up and told her to "move it along." And that was actually almost flattering, because Myra hadn't been wearing a stitch of makeup and was, at that time, at her all-time heaviest.

Her weight: that was one significant detail that her mother had missed. Slowly but inexorably, Myra got bigger and bigger, no matter how little she ate or how vigorously she exercised, power-walking to work and back, gliding maniacally on her Nordic Track, drenched in sweat and breathless. Her weight gain defied all bodily logic. She even had her thyroid tested; the doctor said her thyroid was normal, shaking his head at the enormous anomaly before him.

Thelma hadn't spared Myra the other gory details of Myra's young adulthood, so why had she left out the part where Myra weighed 280 pounds by the age of twenty-six? There was one vague reference:

Quite often, when I aim my vision on you, all I can see is a huge, black, rectangular object, like a filing cabinet.

Myra wore a black leather trench coat all year round. Possibly, if one was seeing via the misty, psychic third eye, one could've mistaken her for a filing cabinet.

Thelma went on and on when Myra was little about the enormous gravity of the psychic gift Myra would inherit. This annoyed Myra, who knew that she had no psychic ability, nor intuition, nor luck: she'd been struck by lightning, twice hit in the head with errant softball bats, bitten by dogs, cats, gigantic ants, a rat, even a babysitter.

This being so, Myra decided as she entered her thirties to make the most of her nonexistent inheritance, and became a seer. She started with neighbourhood people who knew of her mother. In the guise of a social visit, she'd drop in on anxious old women and menopausal shut-ins on disability, and tell them cautiously optimistic things: a lost earring would be found, a shared Bingo win was imminent. She remembered how her mother immersed herself in her subject's situation, laughing and crying with them as though their fate was her own. So Myra piled on the histrionics, mainly to camouflage her lack of insight. She learned quickly that if one was emphatic enough, if one listened with furrowed brow and trembling lip to these ladies, one would immediately become indispensable. It wasn't long before Myra was humbly accepting cash donations, soundlessly sliding tens and twenties into her open purse.

Something else Myra found helpful was the creation of "Spirit," the gabby deity for which Myra was only a mouthpiece. This way she could abdicate all responsibility, and also silence clients bent on further clarification. If Spirit quieted for whatever reason, it would only be rude to press for more prophecy. Clients would go red-faced with shame at having been rude to Spirit.

Myra caught on. In her rustling, tie-dyed coordinates, with her wiry red hair pulled back with a scrunchy, Myra cuddled and comforted the tormented people turning to her for solace and guidance. Of course, Myra's clients had no idea that after each session she went home and threw herself onto the floor, that she yelped and wept at her lack of direction and awful falsity.

+

You'll account for yourself somehow. Some people may consider you unscrupulous. You may consider yourself unscrupulous. Don't worry about it. If you've made it into your thirties, and you've been industrious, and you're not on drugs, and don't have anything venereal, you're probably doing something right. There will be many small happinesses. I can see you sliding nicely through the years until it's time to return to the earth.

With one warning—

One night, after telling a wheelchair-bound woman to be on high alert for a chance encounter with Tom Selleck or at least someone attractive with a moustache, Myra went home and straight to the mirror in her bathroom. She cursed her vast, devious face ("Fucking liar loser fat bitch!"). She pinched and cursed at a blackhead on her greasy cheek ("Cunt cunt cunt cunt! ").

Sobbing, she ordered a large Hawaiian pizza with extra cheese. She ate it in the dark.

She went to bed to scream into her pillow. She got up, took four Benadryls, smoked a joint, and fell asleep across her bed.

When she awoke, she knew only that the day could go two ways: she'd kill herself, or she would try something new, seek out some predictable form of rescue, the first thing she could think of, no matter how corny.

She couldn't think of anything. Clad in a nightie, she donned the leather trench coat and walked to Coffee Time.

En route, she passed the music store: sheet music, all kinds of keyboards, Day-Glo banjos. Myra had never before given the store a second look. Today, though, there was a sign in the window offering, in sparkly cursive, three free guitar lessons with the purchase of an acoustic guitar. And, sitting on a small stool in the middle of the store was a beaming woman with spiky white hair, a guitar on her lap.

Beware a white-haired woman with a friendly face who is either very short or likes to squat like a cave-woman.

Myra bought a guitar for $200. Her aversion to the instrument had suddenly vanished. The high-school hell of drunken boys in their long johns strumming away, butchering "Heart of Gold" in a phlegmy falsetto while she sagged about nude in an old beanbag chair – all of that instantly forgotten.

Myra had no interest in actually learning to play, but here was the white-haired woman for whom she'd been on the lookout. She'd previously thought the white-haired woman was the Golden Griddle waitress who served her once, who she later saw wearing a snowsuit on the subway. But that woman was neither short nor given to squatting. This one here: this was the white-haired woman in question, no doubt about it.

The woman beckoned Myra towards the other, vacant stool. Myra knew that the stool would collapse with her weight, so she squatted above it like a cavewoman. Like a cavewoman!

She will lure you in with the promise of fulfillment, like a child molester uses a chocolate bar to lure a little one into a van. Please, please don't be a dumb Dora about this. The squatting woman will lead you to the edge of madness! Beware this white-haired woman, possibly named Peggy!

"Have you been wanting to learn guitar for a long time?" asked the woman.

"I think so," Myra replied, not really hearing the question.

"I'm so excited for you. You're embarking on a real journey, you really are. My guitar is my best friend. It really is. How much do you know about the guitar?"

"Umm. Nothing."

"Perfect! Let's get started. My name is—"

"Peggy," Myra said.

"How on earth did you know that?"

"I'm psychic. Sort of. Indirectly."

"Oh! Well, that's fun, I guess, eh?"

Myra, she is going to indoctrinate you into a lifestyle, and you'll be thinking, "oh, why not? I live downtown, I vote NDP, I have pierced ears, I know what I'm doing." You do not know what you are doing. You are going to end up with a brush cut and no soul, weeping and wondering why you ever chose sickness over peace.

Peggy showed Myra the parts of a guitar. The head, the frets, the tuning knobs. Myra watched Peggy. She seemed sincere, unencumbered, robust, positive. Myra decided that she was interested in possibly spending the rest of her life with Peggy as Peggy rhapsodized over the G chord: how the G chord changed her life, how all of life's ups and downs can somehow be related back to the G chord, how the G chord is just downright pretty, and who cares if it's the most common chord, we can't all be Joni Mitchell.

Myra asked Peggy if she would share a joint with her.

"Oh my goodness," Peggy said. "I don't know. I haven't smoked pot for ages – almost five weeks now. And I wouldn't want to get in trouble with Ben, the manager. But yeah, sure. There's a parkette right around the corner. Just let me pack up my stuff."

I can't see much beyond this, daughter. I'm not a well woman, and that is my own fault. I accept that responsibility. I smoked like a chimney, laughing all the way, and now I weigh seventy pounds and shit the bed at least once a day. Please think about that before you proceed with that awful, squatting woman. Don't do it. Don't shit the bed of your life.

She walked with her guitar case to the parkette and sat on the lone stone bench there. She checked her pack of smokes for the two pre-rolled joints. She was shivering, either cold or nervous, so she lit up and had a couple tokes.

She would not kill herself today.

acknowledgements

Deepest thanks to:
Barry and Michael Callaghan,
Nina Callaghan, Gabriela Campos, Lisa Foad,
Samantha Haywood, John Webster, Zoe Whittall,
Marc Côté, Joel Cembal, Dick Kearney, Debbie Ward,
Patricia Matte, Debra Matte, Adam Taggart,
Don Oravec, Derek McCormack, Karri and Stan Pelikys,
Mooky Cherian, all at Pink Triangle Press,
and the Black Eagle boys.

I would also like to thank the Ontario Arts Council for a
Writers Reserve grant toward the writing of this collection.

Greg Kearney has published the collection of stories
Mommy Daddy Baby. He lives in Toronto,
and is currently working on a novel.

Author photograph by David Hawe